Book One of th

The Fury

To my wife, love you hun.

Thank you for everything you do for us.

Copyright © 2023 by Joseph Sheehan

All rights reserved. No part of this publication may reproduced, stored or transmitted in any form or by any means, electronic, mechanical, audio, photocopying, recording, scanning, or otherwise without written permission from the publisher. It is illegal to copy this book, post it to a website, or distribute it by any other means without permission.

ISBN: *9798389156173*

First Edition

Table of Contents:

The Beginning

Chapter 1: First Contact

Chapter 2: A Sight to Behold

Chapter 3: A Walk in the Park

Chapter 4: The Blind leading the Blind

Chapter 5: 66 Crescent Road

Chapter 6: A Question, and an Argument

Chapter 7: Caught by the Huntress

Chapter 8: Star Ascending

Chapter 9: The Fury Rose

The Beginning

The first casualty of furniture echoed throughout the house. It was moving day for the new family. A woman jumped, her wearied expression replaced with a look of shock, then annoyance, as she realised her husband had broken something.

Exhausted, she left her toddler in the crib and went to investigate the damage. She did not notice the front door, which hung open by an inch. The toddler had been growing and the crib, an obstacle impossible to climb a few weeks ago, was soon empty.

It had been a strange summer day in the city. Long-term plans were cancelled; few people, if any, went to work, and the roads were all but empty.

A strange day turned to a strange night.

The evening air was warm and sultry, enchanting those few people not already asleep to rest. Sirens occasionally broke the silence of the sleeping city and the light of the moon waxed and waned as a myriad of small clouds jockeyed for position.

Others succumbed to the gentle spell of the fey night, but the toddler became enticed by it. Blue eyes wide, he followed its call. Reaching the front door, he grasped the open edge and pulled. A new world opened before his eyes and little encouragement was needed to walk outside, into the night.

The moon that lulled everyone else to sleep shone a spotlight on the toddler. It pierced the clouds, to focus his attention on a strange pattern, guiding him. Smaller, everyday details leapt into focus: a slug, a flower, two moths who evaded his grasping hands as they flew low over the tarmac drive.

The child followed, laughing as the moths fluttered down the drive and then up to rest on the dim streetlight.

He looked for a moment as if to cry, then, joy. A sparkling bracelet lay on the pavement that someone had dropped earlier that day. All thoughts of moths abandoned, he walked with the unsteady confidence of a toddler towards this newest mystery.

On a journey of a thousand discoveries, which the young make every day, he meandered up the street to the top of the hill. In every sense of the word, he was lost to the larger world around him.

Soon though he began to cry, looking for his mother, tired after the short walk. A glimpse of movement was an answer to his sadness, down the side of the house he sat in front of. He saw hint of a red tail with a white tip. Curiosity led the way, as he still heard the soft call of the night.

Uncertain legs carried him forwards, through the open, iron cast gates. The toddler was rewarded with the sight of a baby red fox limping through a cat flap into the house.

This house had character, standing alone in defiance of two rows of otherwise unbroken terraced houses. Dense yew trees that were placed to shroud the house from its neighbours. Yet even when the clouds overhead cast a deep shadow, the dark timber walls of the house still gleamed as though the light still struck it.

Two tall towers rose out of the spine of its roof. The yew that tried to hide the house could not hide that it was of an odd shape, not so square and regular as the rest of the street. This house that hid from the rest of the street called to the toddler.

And the toddler followed the fox through the cat flap of the house. Soft and silver light emanated from the wooden walls so that it seemed the toddler had crawled into a dim, moonlit daydream.

Inside there was a long corridor with many doors on either side. One end contained a great, wooden table with chairs that were high backed and coated in dust, the other a staircase with railings that swept down from the ceiling.

Floorboards creaked, as the toddler followed the baby fox to the stairs. This staircase led down into darkness and up through the ceiling by an open hatch. The fox went up, and so too did the toddler. Each step was high and made of smooth and worn wood, a trial for one so young. Yet the boy climbed without pause.

As his head poked out of the hatch into a vast beam of moonlight, he cried out and pointed in delight to the front of the house. Where the light poured in through a single plane of glass that was as wide as a man is tall, and so tall as to stretch from the floor to the far distant roof. The walls of the house swept out from the window to gently curve till they reached the houses' full width to eventually square at the back of the long house.

Two vast pillars, in line with the window, broke the light which shone through the glass. They stretched upwards to the peak of the towers seen outside, and each had two circular beams through them. A large telescope sat before the window, pointing to the night sky.

The baby fox had moved towards the back where two short sets of stairs curved upwards. Under the stairs there was an open door where the fox now stood, eyes fixed on the boy. The fox let out a slight whine then limped into the room, and the boy followed.

Under the stairs this wall had an open door, where the fox now stood, eyes fixed on the boy. The fox let out a slight whine then limped into the room. The boy began to walk towards the open door.

It was a sparse cabin, with nothing but a bed, chest, desk, and chair inside, all made from the same dark wood. The fox was lying on the covers of the bed. Bright eyes fixed on the boy; it kept its injured leg cradled in the nook of its body. The only sound in the room was the faint rasp of its breath, as its small chest heaved from exhaustion.

The toddler followed the call which had led him to this room. He made his way to the baby fox, his young eyes wide with natural empathy.

The soft light of the wood became brighter with each step he took towards it. Had anyone else been in the room, they would have felt a faint pressure build in the air. He struggled onto the bed, small legs kicking as he fought for balance.

He made it onto the bed and crawled the last few steps to the fox.

Light emanated from the walls and furniture, to outshine the midday sun and the pressure grew, enough to cause pain.

Yet, the boy and the fox were oblivious to this. As he stretched out his hand to touch the fox, the light and pressure weakened, as if the house itself was holding its breath. The boy reached down to place his hand on the fox's head.

The light flared, blinding, and the pressure became so great as to make the walls and floor creak.

Only for a second.

The light returned to the original dim glow and the pressure disappeared.

The boy and his fox, unaware to the strange events around them, both fell asleep, the boy's arms holding his fox...

The boy's name was James Emerys. Later he was found by his parents on their doorstep, wrapped carefully in a blanket, in a large basket, with a baby fox sleeping next to him.

This is about James, and the fox.

Of course, this must start with her

With velvet fist, she swept my old life away

And chased me into the ether

Where I soared amongst the stars

Sailed amidst giants

And dove into a universe where only possibility remained

That is the Aetherium...

She never was any good at taking no for an answer

Chapter 1: First Contact...

Twelve years later, when James was fourteen, on a Friday evening, after school... A pen is thrown onto a table next to a thick sheaf of homework.

The offending homework was flung up and a brief rain of paper tumbled down onto James's bedroom floor. Reg looked up at him with sympathetic amber eyes. James made to open his bedroom door, to watch TV in the living room. He stopped, trapped. His parents had insisted that he finished his homework this time, no exceptions.

James slumped back down on his seat, unwilling to pick up the papers and pen, so he stared at the open textbook. His hands lifted to cover and rest his head, blocking the book from his sight. *Homework,* he thought, *sucks*.

James sighed and spread his fingers to look through a veil of scruffy hair. Brown eyes, eyes of the earth, Mum said, or mud, according to his friend Freya, rested on The Fury Rose. It was a model ship he and his dad had made a long while back, and James let himself dream instead.

Kerrrrach. James turned to see Reg's long, red body standing on the open windowsill, dragging a claw against the wood. Reg pointed into the evening air with that same paw.

"Don't stand there like that, you're going to fall."

But Reg held his position as a soldier called to attention. It was a curious relationship between owner and pet, one which seemed to attentive observers as being a matter still very much up for debate.

With a poise a gymnast would respect, Reg lowered the paw to scratch another, *kerrrrach*, dragging his claw against the wood before extending his leg and paw out again.

"Really?" James asked.

Reg barked back.

James sighed and pushed himself off the chair, looking to where Reg pointed. It was to a nook of the old oak tree, out of reach from the window. An idea sparked and his eyes, dulled by endless homework, lit with fresh thoughts of freedom.

"Reg, you're a genius."

James crawled under his bed to remove two planks, his long legs sticking out from beneath the untidy covers. Tape was found by trawling through the mess on his desk, which he used to bind the two planks together. James eased them out of the window to be wedged into the nook between two branches.

Reg jumped back onto the windowsill, white, tipped tail flicking from side to side.

James joined him, crouching on the sill, and glanced down from his second-story window. Fear iced his veins, yet muscles tensed by work relaxed with adrenaline and a crooked grin grew. He edged out onto the planks.

Balanced on his hands and knees, James crawled forward. Suspended over thin air, his homework, school, everyday fears became as nothing. All he thought of and all he saw was the next inch.

Coarse bark appeared under his steady hands and the rest of the world came back into focus. James sat on a branch and, for a second, let the stale London air push back his hair and calm his beating heart.

'Hey mate, you free' James texted his best friend, Milo. He knew Milo was free.

Reg trotted over the planks and slipped into his usual position on James's shoulders. Together they climbed down, James picking his way through branches crowned with the bright, green leaves of early summer.

Reg leapt down as James lowered himself onto the tarmac drive. He dusted himself off and walked away, soon winding through Clapham's streets. A left, then right to take a shortcut through the common. Reg at his side and a warm breeze, soon he was lost to his thoughts on the dirt path.

James turned a blind corner around an old, red, brick wall wreathed in ivy, which surrounded Holy Trinity Church in the common, and collided with someone. He tripped over Reg to land hard on his arse.

"You okay?" Brown eyes looked down to meet his own.

"'Course I'm not... I... um," James blushed. "Yeah. I mean, I'm all right."

The callused hand that reached down to grasp his own and the sheer ease with which he was helped to his feet belied the vision that his eyes beheld. Without that first-hand experience, he'd sooner believe that he stood under purple skies and pink grass than lifted like a feather by someone like her.

"Hi," she said, tucking a black lock of hair behind her ear.

"Hi, I..." Words slipped from his mind as she arched an eyebrow his way. "I'm a James."

"A James?" There was a grace to her, James realised, slack-jawed as she tilted her head up in consideration of him. "Perhaps you hit your head harder than I thought."

"I am Artemis."

James imagined the Yangtze River on a clear night in China. Stars lit the scene, reflected on calm waters. Gentle waves lapped the shore near the rows of peach trees in blossom, whose delicate, red flowers graced slight branches, the air fragrant with their scent of honey and almond.

Artemis, James realised, fit that scene. Though by the way she stood, taut and ready to fight or run in flight, she was what was missing from that scene. The moon, as distant and beautiful as the moon.

To reach her, James thought, one must reach the stars.

James realised that he had not said a thing for a long while, and Artemis was still looking at him.

"James, but you knew that. I, ah, sorry for hitting you." Artemis gave James what could only be called an incredulous look.

James spied an oak bench nearby. "Here, why don't I sit down for a second?"

James stumbled slightly on his way to sit. Arse now firmly upon the bench, he saw that Artemis had not moved a muscle as far as he could tell.

"Artemis, you want to sit?"

"You," Artemis said, "are not what I expected."

"We've never met, why would you expect anything?"

"I suppose." Artemis slowly and with a natural grace began to walk to him.

Reg trotted to James, who unconsciously reached to pick him up.

Artemis drew back. "Is that your... pet?"

Reg growled a fox's purr as James stroked his fur. "His name's Reg, short for Reginald. You want to pet him? Unless you've got somewhere to be?"

"No," Artemis said, "I don't have somewhere to be."

"Then why not?"

James smiled and spread his arms out wide. "Evening sun is still shining, the grass is green, and not a drop of rain in the sky. When was the last time you just sat down and watched the world go by?"

Artemis looked at him and Reg, with a caution normally reserved for wild and dangerous animals. Yet his words made her pause and her brow furrowed, and she went to sit on the far end of the bench. She was wearing a jade bracelet, loose on her arm and inscribed with symbols.

"What's that?" James asked.

"This?" Artemis held up her arm with the bracelet upon it. James nodded, and she studied him, curious. "A gift from my mother. It is meant to protect me."

"It's beautiful."

"Thank you." Artemis blinked, and lowered her gaze to see Reg. "What kind of animal is he?"

"He's a fox." James raised his eyebrows. "Have you not seen a fox before?"

"I have," Artemis hesitated, "but…"

"Oh, is English not your first language?"

"No."

"Where are you from? China, Korea, Japan?"

"No." Artemis looked at him with bright eyes, wary still but with an intense curiosity. "Far further away than that."

"Further than that, how? Wait, you don't have to say anything if you don't want to. Sorry."

"Don't be sorry." Artemis smiled, and James would have sworn his heart skipped a beat. "What is it like to live here?"

"In London?" Artemis nodded at his question. "I don't know, it's all right. I grew up here, my friends are here, my family. My primary school ain't far from here either. I don't know all of London that well, I guess, but this bit I do."

"Home," Artemis said, looking around over the green, and at the row of houses beyond. "That I understand."

"I guess it is home."

"I haven't seen my home for a long, long time."

"Really?" James said. "Why?"

"I need to, to 'bring back a treasure to rival any in my father's possession'."

"Wow." James sat back. "That's intense."

"Intense." Artemis laughed for a second, before covering her mouth with a hand. "I can't imagine anyone saying that to him."

"I would," James proclaimed. "I'll say, 'Mate, you're too much. You need to let your daughter come back home without any stupid treasure. Stop being so intense and relax'."

Artemis stared at him, her composure lost with her mouth slightly agape, then she giggled in the first unguarded sound she had uttered. Artemis stopped, astonished that she had done so. She saw James's expression and laughed, so loud as to turn heads. James, by the sheer infectiousness of the sound, soon laughed, too.

"I would say it," James said, after they had calmed.

Artemis leaned close to him. "I believe you," she said.

She studied him now, with the same slight smile as before, if wider and more open.

Reg, nose twitching, woke with a yawning snap. Artemis froze as the fox stood on the bench, sniffed the air, and turned to face her.

"Relax," James said. "It's all right to be nervous, but trust me, Reg is harmless. He is normally shy, but I think he is curious about you."

Reg trotted along the bench to Artemis. He ignored Artemis's wide-eyed stare and how she gripped the arm and back of the chair so hard that her hands were turning pale, and he, somewhat indelicately, curled up on her lap.

"James." Artemis was breathing faster. "Why is he here?"

"He wants you to stroke him."

"What?"

"Stroke" – James mimed it – "on his back. Go on, he won't bite."

"You don't know." Artemis looked down at Reg, then back at James. "You really don't know what he is."

"Reg is Reg." James decided to push past Artemis's occasional strangeness. "He's asleep and you're sitting there like Reg is holding a gun in his paws. Go on, stroke him. Unless you're scared?"

Her nostrils flared at the implication, though she was still gripping the chair despite the fact Reg had been resting quietly on her lap for some time now. Artemis placed a very gentle hand on Reg's fine, red fur and stroked him.

"He's so soft, I did not realise that... foxes could be like this." She smiled, and this time in earnest. "I like his name."

"My dad picked it." James's mouth was dry. "I've had him ever since I could remember."

Her breath caught, and her hand tightened on the scruff of Reg's neck. "I would think that is a very long time for an animal like this to live."

"I'm lucky, I guess."

"You truly don't know..."

James shook his head. This was a strange girl, so strong, so beautiful, and so close, James realised. Reg was all that separated them, and her eyes were as sharp as the arrow of her namesake, searching James's own for some missed comprehension.

"What don't I know?"

"That" – Artemis blinked and moved back, releasing her grip on Reg – "that you really don't know how he's lived so long. I would be curious, aren't you?"

"'Course I am. I don't tell a lot of people about his age, though – worried that someone might take him away."

Reg stirred and kicked against James's leg.

"Don't fret, bud," James said to Reg, picking him up from Artemis's lap. "I'm not going to let anyone take you away from me. You're safe here with me."

"Aren't you worried about me?" Artemis asked.

"You?"

"Yes, me." Artemis seemed almost to crouch, poised on the bench again as though for fight or flight. Something in the way she arched an eyebrow in his direction punctuated her statement as a test to James.

"No?" James, for the record, was not especially experienced at talking to beautiful girls, but this was not what he had been led to expect.

"Careful, James." Artemis looked sad, guilty almost. "Best not to make promises you can't keep."

"What?"

"Close your eyes."

"Okay."

"Now hold out your hand." James did so and felt something cool and sharp land upon it.

"I'll be seeing you, James," she said.

James opened his eyes, and she was gone. He leapt off the bench, Reg tumbling to the floor. In each direction he stared, standing on the bench with one foot high on its back. There were rows of cars and terraced houses, yes. A cat peeing against a car, sure. Of trees and people there were many, but not one with her grace, nor her long, black locks of hair caught by the summer breeze.

"Reg?" James lifted Reg up so they were nose to nose, or nose to snout. "Buddy, did I dream that, and if I did, why does my arse still hurt, and where did I get this?"

James held an arrowhead inscribed with silver.

Reg huffed back, turning his snout up and to the side, ears flicking down. He chuffed in a fox's cough, drew in a sharp breath, and sneezed in James's face.

Chapter 2: A Sight to Behold

James was told to go away and stop 'haranguing' people. He gave up peeking behind trees and under cars in search of Artemis, instead walking the short distance to Milo's house.

He bumped into, nodded to, and said 'evening' to a lamppost while walking across the common. He was so taken by thoughts and questions about Artemis that when a concerned passer-by asked if he was all right, James completely ignored him. The concerned citizen was left shaking his head and questioning out loud about the youth of today, but James's mind was absent from the world.

Milo's house overlooked the common, as neat and orderly as the family who owned it – except for the large garage at the side, Milo's lab and lair, littered with bits, bots, pots, wires, small tires, and a few past fires. And an old Mini that Milo and his dad had restored to near mint condition.

This was to James, Milo, and Freya their nerve centre, the heart of their group.

James banged on the door, and winced as a clatter and clang of falling metal came from inside then muffled swearing. Reg leapt off his shoulders and waited by his side.

Milo opened the door, furiously adjusting his glasses. "James, quiet, you know I'm working on something."

"Something weird happened on the way here." James entered Milo's workshop.

Milo rolled his eyes and followed, ducking so his short afro did not catch on the beams of the ceiling. James snuck a look at Milo's workbench to peek at what he was working on.

"Don't, it's not finished yet." Milo dashed over to cover the parts with an old newspaper. "It's for your birthday."

James huffed, but stepped back, falling into the couch, whose springs creaked in a rusty protest. Reg leapt to his lap and promptly closed his eyes as James stroked his fur.

"All right." Milo sat with altogether more care next to James. "What was so weird?"

James looked down and frowned. He reached out and took a drink out of the mini fridge Milo had installed. After a gulp of orange soda: "Well…"

Bang, a single, loud knock. The door shook.

"Freya?" James asked.

"Yep." Milo walked to the door. "I let her know after you texted me."

"I'm thirsty," Freya said, strawberry curls bouncing as she beelined to the mini fridge.

"How was training?" Milo closed the door behind her, the wind from Freya's passing tugging at his clothes.

"Meh." Freya shrugged. "Dad had me sparring with this black belt visiting from somewhere. He was okay."

Freya dumped her gym bag by the door. She saw James slumped on the couch and frowned, twitching the slight crook in her nose. "What's up with you?"

James looked up from peeling the paper off the cold bottle. "Well..."

"Let's get this straight," Milo said, after James had finished his story. He pushed his thick glasses back with grease-stained fingers. "After escaping your house by walking over a two-story fall like it's nothing, you get the perfect chance to chat to a pretty girl and you're useless. Then, Reg here saves the day... Wish I had a fox."

Reg preened and leapt over to Milo, to comfort Milo with his presence while he napped.

"I don't know." Freya lounged on the couch next to Milo. "Best not make promises you can't keep? Who says stuff like that? And why did you tell her about Reg?"

"Because," Milo said, "James thinks she's pretty."

"Really, James?"

"Well..."

"Bullseye." Milo threw his bottle at the bin. The friends watched it arc up and in. "Right on the money."

"James, James, James." Freya shook her head in mock disappointment as she looked at him.

"What? It wasn't just that." James looked aside and a slight blush reddened his cheeks. "There was something about her."

"Sounds like love." Freya poked him. "Just how hard did you fall over?"

"Classic," Milo said. "I have a stethoscope – perhaps I could see if your heart skipped a beat."

"You and your words," Freya said, nearly growling at having to ask. "What's a stethoscope?"

"The thing doctors use to listen to a patient's heartbeat."

"Right, skipped a beat, funny." Freya laughed. "James is in love."

"I don't love her!"

"Protesting a little too loudly, I think." Milo nodded at his own words, then turned to Freya. "He's a goner."

"We need to meet this girl for ourselves," Freya said. "Check her out before Romeo here gets too head over heels."

"Hey," James said as they laughed, "I'm right here."

"Maybe in body, but" – James did not like the look of that smile on Freya's face – "in your mind I think you and Artemis are sitting in a tree, K-I-S-S-I-N-G."

James buried his head in his hands, as his best friends laughed. He forgot about the arrowhead Artemis had given him. *Better not mention it now,* James thought as Milo cracked another joke, *just be giving them more ammo.* And, in typical English weather, as water began to fall from the darkening sky outside, James threw his empty plastic bottle at Milo only for Freya to catch it mid-air. It was just one of those nights.

...

Later, thunder boomed, and the rain intensified further.

It was near midnight and James looked out of the bus shelter, peering for his ride back home. Dark, heavy clouds had gathered, and poured forth water in a torrent. Light was scarce, as here and there the moon pierced the sky's heavy veil and lightning, striking ever faster, provided brief, if clear images.

Reg howled, high-pitched and keening, as though a ghost had newly awakened and was sounding a dire warning.

James jumped. "Holy... Reg, stop."

James picked Reg up to comfort him, but Reg continued. As his cry rang harsh in James's ear, he raised a paw to point to a patch of clouds.

James knew what this meant and raised Reg higher, so the paw was closer in line with his eye. Reg stopped howling but kept his paw up. The line of his paw shifted, tracking something in the night sky. Lightning flashed and thunder boomed, the light painting a picture.

James nearly dropped Reg, there was something in the clouds. Something huge, and certainly not a bird, nor a plane.

Lightning and more thunder, and this time James did drop Reg. It was a ship, a wooden ship, silhouetted against the cloud and with its sails pushed taut.

Reg pawed at his jeans and James hurried to pick him up again. Reg raised his paw and James cocked his head to follow the paw's slow movement. Reg pointed to the moon and the clouds did part.

Wrapped in an ethereal shroud, the ship looked to be taken out of a time centuries ago. The vessel was fashioned of graceful curves of dark wood. Three masts with three square sails adorned its deck with a jib tied to a long jutting prow. Its back, the stern, was raised by another floor and people, tiny figures, rushed over its deck and rigging.

Then it was gone, hidden behind another cloud. Reg howled again for a few brief seconds and lowered his paw.

Slack-jawed, James stared towards the heavens.

"Oi, mate!" James started. "You wanna stare at clouds or you wai'ing for the bus?"

He spun to see yellow light spilling out of an open bus door, the driver's cragged face leering at him.

"...What?" James said.

"You in, kid, or you out?" Thunder boomed, and James flinched, glancing up.

"In."

With one last look, he entered the bus. He paid for the journey and took a seat, ignorant of the driver's curious stare.

Chapter 3: A Walk in the Park

James was taking Reg out for a walk. A chore for sure, but it was the only way to get out of the house being grounded after last night's adventure. With Reg being a fox, this walk, along with most of their walks, was at night. Not proper dead of night, as it was London and according to his parents' 'not safe'. Nor day as foxes prefer the night. Twilight then, agreed on by James, Reg, and his dad.

Besides James quite liked twilight, when the hush of night began to fall, and the stars would peek out after a day's rest.

His shoes occasionally scuffed the grey pavement. Houses and clouds were clad in that red-orange wash that sometimes comes with the fading sun. The full moon was visible by day and brightened further as James and Reg turned left to walk their favourite street before Clapham Common: Crescent Way, a crescent by the line the road followed, too.

What sold it to Reg, or so James thought, was the smells. Head turning, nose twitching smells, plucked from around the world. Walk down this street around dinner time and it seemed to James that half of Earth's cuisine could be sampled by just smell. Rich curries with exotic spices from one house, fried droolworthy chicken from another, Italian and, Reg barked, drooling, a flaming beef brisket barbeque.

For James, it was the house at the apex of the crescent of the road. 66 Crescent Way, tucked away and hidden, seeming to have retired behind a shroud of yew trees. Yew symbolised death, life, and resurrection and was short compared to other trees, with leaves better called needles, soft and green in every season.

To James's eye, terraced houses often seemed like soldiers standing to attention, establishing perfectly ordered streets. But here, on an almost perfectly ordered street, there was an odd duck hidden amidst the swans. 66 Crescent Way, sandwiched right and left by ranks of soldiers disapproving of this scrag-muffin of a house.

The house had not a single straight line to it; indeed, it curved from its back out to a fatter middle and swept in till the front was a bare metre across. A great window dominated that narrow front, a single pane of glass that stretched from the bottom of the first floor to the roof. Behind that glass the house was always dark.

The house had to be haunted, Freya told him, before promptly betting him to knock on its front door.

James won the bet.

The front gate had squealed on rusted hinges that night. A younger James had slipped into the front garden and passed the yew. The great window loomed over him, able to hide any number of eyes behind it. James flinched under the high, dark door raised atop stairs of weathered stone, and shivered under the dark wood of the house that gleamed too clearly on that cloud-ridden night. He froze, he thought he saw something move behind the window.

Reg had been there, urging him forward.

Moss squelched underfoot; his breath billowed out as steam. James dared the climb. One foot forward, then the other. From the top step he shifted his weight forward, hand outstretched to grasp the door knocker. Ready to run. He'd grasped the cold metal. Lifted it, slammed it down before running out the gate and sprinting down the street. Freya and Milo at his heels from where they had been waiting outside the gate.

An older, and certainly no wiser, James stood outside the house again. He liked scrag-muffins, oddities and mysteries, and the house was mystery enough to make the other mysteries of the world seem a bit more real.

James turned away with Reg — a mystery for another day, though.

Something moved behind the long window on the first floor. Bright eyes peeked out, tracking James and Reg down the road.

The road curved on, and soon the end was in sight. Trees popped into view as Clapham Common emerged. Streetlights illuminated this busier road before the green. The wind from a passing lorry tugged James's clothes, as he hop-stepped to cross the road quickly between a gap in the cars. James and Reg paused on the other side, a few steps inside the green grass of the common. The orange streetlight faded, so that the green had a dim, silvered tone from what natural light shone from above.

"The stars are bright tonight, aren't they, lad?"

"What?" James turned.

Silver haired, with skin weathered enough to resemble bark, the man who'd spoken chuckled. He sat on a worn, wood bench facing the green common. He was not tall, nor short. Most folk became frail as they aged, but he was among those who aged like leather. An old, salty sailor, pipe wagging as he spoke.

"The stars." A hand lifted from the gnarled staff it rested on, to point up. "They call to a person, don't they?"

"I guess? I'm… Reg."

Reg had leapt up on the bench and rested his head on the old man's thigh. The man, seeing a fox on his lap, simply smiled and stroked his fur as Reg purred.

"Reg, Reg, get over here." Reg yawned, snapping his teeth before settling his red head down again.

"It's all right, lad." The man's smile creased his dimples and deep wrinkles gathered around pale, blue eyes. "He's not troubling me."

"Sorry, he's my pet and… Reg, get over here." Reg huffed and batted a hind leg James's way. "He's normally shyer around strangers."

"Is he now? Seems friendly to me."

"Well, yeah, not today, but normally he's shy." Shy was an understatement. James felt it was more accurate to say Reg was a blooming ghost when he felt like it.

"Are you a fox whisperer or something?" James asked.

"Fox whisperer." The man smiled. "No, though animals do seem to like me. Say, are you and Reg here venturing around the park for a walk?"

"Yeah, you could say that."

The man, with a care most reserved for children, lifted Reg off his lap and placed the fox beside him.

"Good, good," the old man said, his walking staff grinding against the gravel as the man pushed himself up. "Me, too. The path is dark, and company would be welcome."

Reg leapt off the bench and to James's side. He pawed at the boy's trousers and whined, big, amber eyes gazing up at him.

"Reg, you don't have to do that. I was going to say yes."

James caught sight of the old man's raised eyebrow, watching him have an argument with a fox.

The man said nothing though. Together they started to walk, dirt path scuffing under their feet.

Idle conversation flourished as they wound their way through the common. Mostly the old man, his gnarled staff thud-thudding against the ground, spoke of the stars. He named constellations as you might old friends. James pointed to random stars to test him, but the man would smile and nod, before offering a story or fact about each one.

A conversation with some rare people is akin to sitting in front of a warm fire with a cup of tea, after a long and cold day. Such folk are often old with wrinkles best understood when they smile, who find joy in the simple fact of being alive and impart a feeling that you can speak without judgement.

This old man was among those rare people.

"I just finished school, so I'm happy about that, too."

"Aye?"

"Yeah, school, school's like knowing what I'm meant to say, but knowing what I want to say. And if I don't say what I'm meant to say, I get in trouble."

"Afraid to say, lad, but you might find it to be little different when you're older."

"Really, that sucks. Those looks" – James kicked a rock to send it bouncing across the ground – "they make me want to stop talking altogether."

"Enjoy the time you're at, lad. Ain't easy, but that's my piece on it anyway." The man blew a smoke ring from his pipe. "What about your friends? Imagine they won't mind what you say."

"I am not exactly popular... Hey, what's your name again?"

"Aye, I never did introduce myself, did I?" The old man smiled. "I'm Giles."

"Giles." James nodded, the name did fit him. "I'm James."

"Pleasure to meet you, James." Giles held out a hand.

James stared at the offered hand for a second, before he realised what it was and rushed to shake it. Giles's hand was coarse and tough to the point James thought it felt more like wood than skin.

"Pleasure to meet you, too, Giles."

"You were saying that you weren't popular," Giles said, as they started to walk again.

"No. I do have friends, though. Two good friends really, Milo and Freya. Three, if you count Reg."

"I think Reg most definitely counts. Milo and Freya, have they been with you through thick and thin?"

"Yeah, without doubt." Reg purred, rubbing against James's leg.

James picked Reg up, holding him so he could crawl to rest around James's shoulder as though to mirror a living, breathing scarf.

"Lad, I can tell you that two or three friends that you trust is something far more precious than a hundred you doubt."

Silence followed, resting comfortably between them for the next few minutes. A slight wind caused the leaves and branches to creak and whisper, and moonlight bathed the grass and trees. Bats flickered by, and in the distance a man huffed and puffed as his dog pulled him along. James shifted Reg on his perch so his fox's breath would not blow straight into his nose.

"Is he not heavy?" Giles asked.

"Reg? Nah, you get used to that. It's not the weight, but his breath — a fox's breath stinks."

Reg cracked open an eyelid at that. He flicked his white-tipped tail into James's face, waving as though to sweep the words out of James's mouth.

"Reg, Reg, stop it or I'm putting you down."

Reg huffed, tail settling down. But as a parting gift, he blew a warm, sour breath into James's face.

"Reg, that is foul, mate."

"Aye," Giles laughed, "you have a special bond there, lad."

"Yeah? Smelly bond, more like. Reg, we need to brush your teeth again."

Giles's laughter rolled out over the common green, a touch of warmth in the cooling night.

"James." Giles paused to take a deep, satisfied breath and a long look up at the stars. "I think it is time for me to head back home and to sit in front of a fire with tea. These ancient bones of mine appreciate time at home."

"All right, me and Reg can help see you back."

"Now that is a kind offer, lad. This way, I make berth at 66 Crescent Way, close to where we started."

"66 Crescent Way, the haunted house?" James blushed. "My, my friend Freya says it's haunted, I... sorry."

"It does look strange compared to the rest of the street." Giles smiled, and starlight twinkled in his eyes. "But strange does not always mean bad. No, sometimes strange can be something extraordinary."

James and Giles turned off the dirt path, the old man's staff tapping on the new tarmac.

"Do you wonder, lad," Giles asked, "if there's anything up there?"

"Up where?"

"There." Giles cocked his gnarled staff up, aiming through the thick branches of the trees above and up at the stars.

"What, in space?"

"Aye." And the word spoke as though it weighed as iron.

"Sometimes." James slowed. "Why?"

Reg shifted, amber eyes trained on Giles, who stopped, and it seemed the weight of his own question now fell back on him.

A weight Giles greeted with a straightened back, as though an ancient oak, strong and deep rooted in the face of a hurricane storm. And those whom might meet his gaze would see a fire that did more then merely warm the soul. There was power there, clear as the stars above, and bright behind his kind eyes.

"Would that we had more time lad, that I could say this in a kinder fashion. Destiny, is lying on your shoulders."

"Lying on my... What, you mean Reg?"

"Yes, don't you wonder why Reg has never aged? How you and he talk like you do?"

"A little, but he's my friend." James stepped back and shook his head. "That's all I want him to be. And how do you know he's never aged?"

"Lad, I will not lie, Reg is..." Giles frowned, then his staff snapped on guard as the fox growled.

A slim figure approached with graceful strides, a shadow in the twilight. His or her face was concealed by a porcelain white mask. Behind that figure loomed a giant. The two paused, and the figure gestured for the man behind to step forward.

So the giant of a man approached, bald and covered in a black coat. His skin gleamed softly under the bright night like polished ebony. He stopped in front of them, looking down at them with thick corded arms folded and tree-trunk legs spread apart. The path ahead was blocked.

"Her Highness wishes to avoid unpleasantries." His voice reverberated like boulders down an alpine slope. "You will give me what she desires, and we will be on our way."

As he spoke, men emerged from the dark to surround them. Their faces were often scarred and grim, if not obscured by deep hoods entirely.

James froze as the men drew long blades from under their coats. A car beeped from the road far away, the sound echoing to where James, Reg and Giles now stood surrounded by swords and a giant.

Giles sighed. The giant blinked as the men holding the swords shifted. No man should sound so relaxed with so many naked blades so near.

"I'm sorry, James" – Giles looked at James and Reg – "but it has already begun."

James stared back, palms sweaty and voice hoarse. "What?" he managed.

"Enough," the giant said, "take them."

The circle of sharpened blades tightened as the men closed the gap between them. Giles raised his staff high, and light pooled in the crevices and whorls of the wood. The staff and the light within shone as a beacon in the dark common.

"No!" The giant lurched forward as Giles slammed the staff into the ground.

Reality warped. A shockwave of light erupted from the impact, and James knew no more.

...

Threads of his mind were pushed apart as though by a violent wind. A feather's impact on Earth. His thoughts coalesced and James saw the world enriched in swirling silver-blue currents. A ghostly sea of blue-silver flame. The currents mixed, twisted, danced together as though air was fire with no ending or beginning. Tongues of flame stretched endlessly, through him, in him. James could not tell whether they best represented fire or water.

The currents, the fire, intertwined most densely when passing through an object. Be it the trees, the occasional lamp post, or even the individual blades of grass, it was there and ever in motion. To James, it was as a veil lifted from his sight.

The last he saw before this faded was a tree. Bright and crowned in life and glory. Leaves as tongues of fire, and its trunk a deep well of blue-silver light. That light swelled from its roots and was held deep within its cragged bark. A blaze, a bright luminescence poured out of the tree's myriad leaves in a crackling and shimmering halo.

What more glorious sight was there to see, than the true nature of a single tree.

And then it was just a tree, halo extinguished, blue-silver light vanished, the bark coarse and its brown lines dim.

"What, what was that? Giles?" James was sitting on a bench. The same bench at which he had first seen Giles, except this time there was not a car, nor person, nor Reg in sight.

"Reg, Giles?"

James stood, unsteady legs carrying him to the tree he had seen wreathed in blue-silver. His hesitant hand shivered before touching the bark. James flinched back, but nothing. The bark was simply that, bark, and rough beneath his touch.

"What is going on? Was that real, Giles, Reg?"

An airplane rumbled overhead, a siren wailed in the distance, and someone closed a window, intent on ignoring James's cries. Normal, everyday London sounds.

A black cat leapt atop a nearby car and stretched, claws scritch-scratching through the car paint, eyes gleaming. A high-pitched bark, and the cat hissed as Reg raced past. Reg howled as he ran straight into James's arms with enough force to knock him to the ground.

"Reg." The fox licked his face again and again . "Reg, stop, I'm okay, I'm okay."

James held Reg up with both hands. "Buddy, we need to brush your teeth again."

Reg barked, wagging his tail.

James sat up, one knee to the ground, and stroked Reg's fur. "I'm so happy to see you, buddy. What happened back then, was that all even real?"

A scuff, a slight scrape and Reg's head snapped round, teeth bared and growling. James yanked his hand back, scrambling to his feet. Memories of sharpened steel caught his breath. The black cat walked out from behind the car, and Reg huffed. It hissed at Reg once more, and Reg barked, causing it to run.

"Reg?" The fox continued to stand alert, a low growl emanating from his chest.

"Reg?" James stepped forward, a twig cracking beneath his feet. Reg spun around and lunged, teeth snapping down on thin air as James whipped his hand back. James stared, holding his hand back. Reg had never done anything like that before. Reg whined and backed away, legs bent and head shaking.

"Reg, Reg, it's okay." James inched forward, kneeling, and placed a hand on Reg's red furred back. "I'm fine, see?"

Reg sneezed, letting James gather him in his arms. As James stood Reg sneezed again on James's shoulder.

"Let's go home, Reg," James said, stroking his red fur. "Let's go home, buddy."

Chapter 4: The Blind Leading the Blind

A long, rough tongue rasped against James's neck and up along his cheek, leaving a trail of saliva.

"Reg, stop it."

James woke to see familiar amber eyes. He turned over to escape the attempt to wake him. Reg, determined in his pursuit, clambered over James and continued.

"All right, I'm up, I'm up, Reg." James stretched, twisting and back cracking. He yawned, sat up and rubbed his eyes.

"Every morning," James said.

Clothes were piled in mounds dotted around the room, which James affectionately called his 'floor-drobe'. He glanced outside to see the old oak, leaves fluttering in the wind. James remembered last night, the magic, dire threats by swords, and Giles. Time trickled past, till Reg nudged him with his nose.

"Did all that really happen, Reg?" The fox huffed and placed a paw on James's lap. "Last night, I mean."

Reg whined, then leapt to place his back paws on James's legs and his front paws on James's chest, the fox's eyes level with James's own. James had to place a hand back to support the weight.

His amber eyes were fierce, large so close to James's brown, and a soft growl came from deep in Reg's chest.

"It was real," James said, "but how?"

Reg's head jerked back, a whine escaping. He leapt off James's lap. A bark, and Reg trotted out of the bedroom.

James walked out of the door and to the bathroom where Reg was waiting, bushy tail flicking from side to side. After a steaming shower and a brief and somewhat successful attempt to brush Reg's teeth, James set to work on his own teeth in front of the mirror.

"Not, not handsome." James remembered what Freya had said once. Freya didn't do praise well, but in her own way, she had been trying to be nice. "I'll be seeing you around, James… That's what Artemis said, Reg."

"I can't be that bad then." *She had been beautiful, which meant he couldn't be that bad.* James nodded at the thought; the logic checked out to his mind.

Milo, if he had been there and part of the conversation, would have nodded back. Freya would likely call them both idiots. James frowned at that thought, then shrugged. "You think I'll see her around, Reg?"

Reg shook his head before spitting out the last of the toothpaste into the shower and glared at James.

"Don't be like that. Come on, I bet Mum and Dad will cook us some sausages for breakfast."

James checked his phone while yawning. To his surprise, it was filled with messages. Curious about this, he unlocked it.

"Crap, my own birthday…"

In record time, he made it downstairs. Mouth-watering smells awaited – a cooked English breakfast – and the radio was loud. His parents waited for him in the living room, not too shabby, nor too neat. It was filled with knick-knacks and two well used sofas pointed at the TV in the corner. A small fireplace boasted a small mantel, where sat a ramshackle selection of family portraits, interspersed with flowers. There was an open view to the family kitchen, with a long counter to separate the two.

Dad held his watch up, lowered his glasses, and peered at the time displayed. James, who had seen this gentle exaggeration many times before, dipped his head and dropped his eyes.

With a faint smile, Dad said, "You do remember agreeing to wake up early so you can open your presents with us? Before your mum and I have to leave?"

"Yeah, sorry about that," James said with a half-smile, and a hand pushed through scruffy hair. "I did wake up in time though."

"Meaning that Reg once again woke you up on time. He's a fox, James, not an alarm clock."

"I don't know, why can't he be both? He does a pretty good job at being an alarm, plus he's got the whole fox thing down." James stroked Reg's head.

"James, don't be so sarcastic," said Mum. "Happy fourteenth birthday."

Meanwhile, next to the table Dad was once again trying to get Reg to eat dog food, this time while wrapped up in a thin slice of raw bacon.

"Dad, give it a rest." James grinned and pulled out two chairs around the kitchen table before sitting. "When has he ever fallen for your tricks?"

"I've given up trying to explain that fox," Dad said. "You know the story of how you vanished as a baby. Then reappeared on our doorstep, in a basket of all things, with him sleeping next to you."

"I know, Dad, everyone knows."

"I've had to tell the veterinarian we've got a new fox twice now. They're not supposed to live for twelve years." Dad glared at Reg as if expecting the fox to provide the answer right then and there. Reg took the seat next to James, yawned and slumped down on the chair as James scratched behind his ears.

"James!" Mum snapped. "How many times do I have to tell you, Reg can't sit on the chairs?"

"But Mum" – James and Reg looked at her with wide, pleading eyes – "it's my birthday."

"Fine." She threw up her hands and laughed. "Just stop that. It's not nearly as convincing as when you were babies."

They ate, and the radio turned to the news in the background.

"Local news – last night there was a disturbance at Clapham Common. Arriving at the scene, police found what they called 'a giant of a man' unconscious, along with several others. Police reported that they were armed with swords and were cuffed as they slept. Upon waking the giant refused to identify himself and apparently 'broke out of his cuffs like a superman' before escaping with the rest of the men... Jeff, you sure about this? Swords? Right, let's move on to other, more serious, news."

"James, James," Dad said, "you okay, son? What's got your face working like that?"

"Nothing, just gas, bad stomach."

James gulped down the rest of his food, keeping an ear on the radio. But the radio team, evidently deciding to check the facts again, never mentioned it. Soon James was helping Dad carry the suitcases to the car.

"Remember," Dad said to James as the last suitcase was stuffed inside, "I expect the house to be standing when we get back."

"Why wouldn't the house be standing?"

"I don't know." Dad winked. "That's what worries me."

"Hilarious, Dad."

"Food is in the fridge and if you need any help, don't hesitate to call. Remember to call us from Milo's. You did organise that for the next couple of nights didn't you James?" His mum said, after a hug.

"Yeah, don't worry about it." James said.

With that they were off, leaving James alone. As soon as his parents were out of sight of the doorway, he rushed back inside, grabbed his phone and sent a text to Milo and Freya.

'Parents have left, want to come over?'

...

Dring, dring, the doorbell rang. James finished the last piece of lunch and went to open it.

"James." A huge grin threatened to split Milo's face. "Happy birthday!"

Reg leapt out of the kitchen to greet Milo.

"Reg!" Milo said, holding the fox back. "How are you? Calm down! Here, here, I got a gift for you, too."

As Reg gnawed and slobbered over his birthday bone, Milo cleaned his thick-rimmed glasses of fox spit with his sleeve before he passed James his present.

"This is what I was making yesterday." Milo pushed his glasses up the bridge of his nose. "I know your parents won't get you one, so I made one for you instead."

"That has to be one of the best things you can hear before getting a present." James tore the packaging off to reveal a BB gun.

Polished wood and burnished metal, the BB gun was made to look as though it was used by pirates.

"Damn, mate." James held it to the light. "I have no idea how you make this stuff."

"That's not the best bit."

"What's better than a BB gun?"

"I thought if I made one," he said, and he turned out his coat to reveal the inside, "making two is not that much harder."

...

"I won't lose, not again."

"James," Milo said, "are you sure we should do this again?"

"Yeah, I want to win one."

"We could be here a then."

James crouched down behind the couch. He checked the cartridge, one pellet left. James strained to hear anything, wishing his heart would not beat so loudly. "How many pellets do you have left?"

"One."

"Same," James said. "On three?"

"On three."

"One." James pictured Milo rising from behind the kitchen counter.

"Two." He forced himself to breathe.

"Three!" James stood, ready to finish this once and for all.

James felt the sting as Milo's shot hit. James aimed and squeezed the trigger. *Dring, dring*, the doorbell. He missed Milo by the barest inch.

The plastic bullet ricocheted around the kitchen. It hit pots and pans in a chorus of metallic pings. It knocked a bottle onto the floor, which shattered, before ending its flight by plunging into a small bag of flour. This tore and spilt its contents onto the tiled floor to mix with the drink and broken glass.

Both teenagers stood there for a few seconds. Milo broke the silence. "I told you this was a bad idea. Your mum is going to kill us... you. Your mum will kill you, not me. This was not my fault."

"Only if she finds out." James winced, picturing her reaction. He turned his eyes from the small scene of devastation.

"Well, look on the bright side." Milo smiled. "At least I won."

In mock fury, James pointed his gun at Milo who ducked behind a couch. Before anything else could occur, the doorbell rang again. This time it went on for some while, the patience of the ringer having vanished.

Over the loud ringing of the doorbell, Milo and James looked at each other. "Freya's here."

James left the kitchen for a moment, with its increasingly large puddle of drink and flour, and opened the door.

"You know," James said, "you could wait a bit longer before you start ringing the doorbell non-stop."

Freya rolled her eyes. "Or you could just answer the door quicker." She tossed her black jacket onto a peg and strode into the hall.

"Oh yeah." Freya turned back. "Happy birthday, James."

She gave him a birthday card. James opened it to find money.

"Figured this way you could get what you want," she said. "Where's Reg?"

"Somewhere outside," James said as they walked into the kitchen. "He'll be back in a bit."

Freya frowned. Reg was one of Freya's few soft points. "Got anything to drink? I'm thirsty."

"Yep." James bit back a grin. "It's just about everywhere in the kitchen."

Freya continued to stride through the living room where she said hi to Milo. Her momentum was stopped by the chaos in the kitchen.

"When you said the drink was everywhere, you meant everywhere."

"Yep, you want to help clean up?" James asked.

"Nope."

She helped herself to a drink from the fridge. "To be honest, I'm surprised you haven't managed to burn the house down at some point in your life."

"I'm not that bad." James thought back to his dad's parting words.

"Remember that time we were having a barbeque," Milo said, "and it started to drizzle so you moved it under the tree. Then you went inside and forgot about it."

"That was five years ago, and the tree didn't look that bad afterwards," James said. "How about when you caused that accidental smoke bomb in the chemistry lab? We had to run before Mr Havisham could see it was us."

"I was testing a theory I had," Milo laughed, "which was your idea. It was funny though."

Freya jumped over the large puddle of drink, flour, and shattered glass. "Are you planning to clean this up, James? It smells here now."

"Yeah." James sniffed the air and grimaced. "I guess I should. Does smell a bit."

James left to find a mop whilst behind him he heard Freya laugh as Milo told her about the shootout they'd had. Milo's description of how the mess was caused left her laughing with glee.

"Well" – James swept the glass as Reg trotted back in from the garden – "I guess this is one way to have a birthday, right, buddy?"

Reg barked and leapt onto the counter, nudging the radio with his nose.

"I was going to tell them after this." James shook the mop, drops of water flying.

"Tell us what?" Freya called out.

"Well," James said, "something crazy happened during Reg's walk last night."

"On the common?" Milo asked. "James, I have shown you the numbers. Considering the number of times you and Reg have walked through the common at night, it was only a matter of time before you got mugged."

"You got mugged?" Freya said. "You look all right. I would have fought back."

"No, I wasn't mugged, not really." James cocked his head to one side. "I think."

"You think you were mugged?" Milo turned off the TV as both he and Freya gave James their full attention.

"James, what happened?"

"Last night, it was weird. I don't know where to start." Reg padded around the top of the counter to nuzzle James's arm as he took a long breath and a deep drink of a fresh bottle.

"All right, I guess I should start when I met this old guy called Giles..."

James had his eyes closed as he finished. He told them the end, too, and heard himself say it. Sounded like a fairy tale, a sham, pure fiction.

"Yeah," Freya said. "If I didn't know you better, I'd be calling you a liar right now."

"You believe me?" James said. "I'm not sure I believe me, and it happened to me."

"Yeah, you said it happened, so it happened, and if it didn't, I'll box your ears in. I don't know about the end, but something did happen 'cause I know you. You wouldn't lie about something like this. Easy."

"Thanks." James smiled – that was the most Freya-like sentence he'd heard in a while. "Milo?"

"James, I like logic. That story can't be real." James waited. He knew Milo had more to say and so, for once, did Freya. "But you mentioned that the story was on the radio. I checked on social media and here. Look, something happened."

James leant out, still sitting on the counter, to snatch the phone Milo held over the back of the couch. The phone screen was filled with stories of an explosion of light during the night, confused police reports and a few photos of the scene of the crime.

"This is it – looks a bit different during the day, but yeah, I think that is where me and Giles were."

"It is worth noting, that this is the second such odd story you have told us in as many days, with both Artemis and Giles seeming to take an interest in Reg."

"You're right," James said, and the friends turned to look at Reg. Who was gnawing at his birthday bone again, slobbering on the counter.

"Why though?" Freya said. "Look at him. He's a fox."

"Perhaps, but most foxes only live till they are six. You've had Reg for twelve and he doesn't even look old."

"Guys, Giles asked me if I'd ever thought about how me and Reg communicated so well."

"What are you thinking, James?" Milo asked.

"That we have to go to 66 Crescent Way, where Giles lives."

"No, we don't," Milo said. "If your story is true, there are people, dangerous people, looking for you and Reg. We should stay right here and let the police find them."

"Plus" – Freya shifted on the couch – "66 Crescent Way, that place is haunted. And don't give me that look, Milo, everyone knows it. Why would we go there anyway?"

"It's not haunted." James leapt off the counter. "Giles lives there."

"So, the magic man from last night lives there, so what? Doesn't make me want to go there."

"Means it's not haunted though."

"Maybe." Freya turned her head away and shrugged.

"I'm right, and Giles is here to help." James now stood before them and the TV, one hand gesturing, tone helping him paint the vision of his words.

"Milo, what if it's Reg they want? We can't do anything to stop them."

"James…"

"And they found me and Reg in the middle of the night in a dark park. What if finding us isn't hard for them?"

"You do not know that for certain." Milo's power, his intellect, was beginning to fail, though, retreating like high cliffs under the erosion of countless waves.

"But what if they can find us? And Freya, what's your dad always saying?"

"The best defence is a good offence."

"Magic old men, gangs with swords. Somehow, they found me and Reg in the middle of the park at night. Right now, they've got us on the back foot. We need to know what is going on, and the only person who knows is Giles."

"Freya," Milo said, not liking the familiar gleam in her eyes, "this isn't a martial arts tournament."

"Yeah, well, this definitely ain't a science fair either, so don't give me that." Freya sat forward, and in her eyes gleamed a fierce and certain knowledge. "James is right, someone is picking on us. And I'm not going to sit on my but waiting for the next time."

"Exactly." James stepped forward. "We've got to know more, Milo."

"I, but... Reg." Milo was perhaps becoming a little desperate. "Reg, you want to stay here. I gave you the bone, don't bite the hand that feeds you. Let's make the vote even: two against two."

Reg nuzzled Milo's foot, stood, leapt off the couch and barked before trotting to the front door.

"Sorry Milo," James said. "You're outvoted."

Chapter 5: 66 Crescent Way

The drizzle made Reg wrinkled his long snout and the three friends wrapped up in warm, rainproof coats to keep the damp cold out. It was a just that sort of day, as they walked to 66 Crescent Way.

"Milo," James asked, opening the backpack Milo had asked him to hold, "why did you bring the BB guns?"

"Because I don't believe in haunted houses, ghosts or spirits," Milo said. "But how would you put it? The house does look creepy."

"It's haunted," Freya said. "Stop jinxing it."

"Sure." Milo said, as they stopped at a set of lights. "I'll leave you with your superstitions. Besides, if you are so certain it is 'haunted', why did you want to come?"

"I can't see Giles living in a place that's haunted," James said. "He said the house was strange, but strange can sometimes be something extraordinary."

"What does that even mean?" Milo asked.

"Look," Freya said, "it means that not all houses that are haunted, are haunted by evil things. They can be haunted by good stuff, too."

"Right, and pigs will be flying down Oxford Street any day now."

The argument continued and James would have jumped in on Milo's side, but for the events of last night. To James it seemed, almost, as if, all that was once certain, was now in doubt. They turned onto Crescent Way, a car stalling on the road ahead of them. It was quiet; grey clouds a dark shroud overhead, behind which the Sun slumbered, and the winds a whisper.

"Haunted houses do not exist."

"You've just jinxed this massively, again."

"I hope not," James said, "'cause we're here."

Grey was the day, and odd the house. An odd, ugly duck of a house, seemly shunned by a very English orderly street it resided in.

The three of them peered through the veil of unkempt yew trees, glimpsing the dark wood which seemed too bright for the day's poor light.

"Yep," Freya said, "told you this place is haunted."

"I don't know, it feels familiar now, somehow," James said in a soft voice. To him it seemed like an old, forgotten memory.

"James." Milo shook his head. "The only thing that's familiar about this house is the fact it has a door."

"Come on" – James opened the gate – "let's take a look."

James stepped in with Reg. Neither Milo nor Freya followed.

"James" – Milo glanced across to Freya – "don't you think this place is a little… eerie, not haunted, just, yeah, eerie."

"No." James tilted his head to one side. "If anything, the opposite."

"James" – Freya stressed each word – "it's creepy as hell."

James hesitated and took a step back, then Reg barked.

James looked back to see Reg on the small pathway around the side of the house to the door. A dim memory surfaced: of a small and injured baby fox, waiting for him at that exact spot.

James put a hand to his head. Not in pain, no, that sense of familiarity was back and with it, warmth. Warmth akin to those moments when meeting an old friend.

"It won't take long, come on." James walked through the gate, past the shroud of trees to follow Reg.

Milo shouldered his bag and readjusted his glasses.

"Haunted houses don't exist," and he followed James in.

"For God's sake." Freya bounced on her toes. "If Milo and James can do it, no doubt I can."

And Freya marched forwards after her friends.

James paused, past the trees. A single window dominated the narrow front of the house, from the bottom of the first floor and ending under the roof. A single sheet of glass, dark from the lack of light behind it, and near two storeys high.

Reg ignored this, trotting down the path which curved alongside the house. James trailed behind, noting the only other windows existed on the ground floor and were small and circular. The door awaited them at the apex of the curve.

"What are you doing?" Milo said as Freya approached. "On you go, knock already."

James rapped his knuckles against the wooden door. The rap faded, then echoed inside. Echoed a second too late, and louder than it should. The house seemed to shiver, and dust did fall from the eaves over the door.

"Well," Milo said, after a few seconds, "seems like no one is in. We should go."

Reg slipped through the cat flap. The friends paused.

"What now?" Freya asked.

"Reg isn't afraid to go inside," James said, softly.

"We could wait for Reg to come back." Milo pushed his glasses back and nodded.

"We have to," Freya said. "We don't have the key."

James tilted his head to one side. He reached out and pushed. The door swung open. Inside was an unadorned entrance leading to a corridor stretching lengthways down the house.

"Or," Milo swallowed, "you could do that."

"James." Freya tried to place a restraining hand on his shoulder.

But without a second thought, James was already off. Freya clenched her fists, her features set to a determined expression, and went in. Milo pushed his glasses back, and stepped foot into the dim light.

James pressed onwards, pursuing the small paw prints left in the thin coat of dust on the floor. He turned right down the corridor to see Reg waiting by the staircase at the far end. Reg pawed the steps leading down. He wanted James to follow.

"Let's split up. I'll see what Reg is up to, you guys search the rest of the house," James called out behind him – he did not want to give them the chance to stop him. That pull on his heart was an ache, one James would not ignore. So, he followed Reg down the stairs.

...

Without James, a sense of unease, of being watched pressed upon Milo and Freya. It intensified then dropped, as if the house had decided to tolerate their presence. Milo released a deep sigh and was gratified to see Freya do the same.

Catching Freya's eye, Milo managed a smile. "Ladies first?"

"Lady?"

"Fine, martial arts champ first."

"Better."

Freya bent her knees and walked forward as she would in the fighting ring. In that way, with this floor's low ceiling and dim light, she peered into the first of many small rooms along the corridor. Each one felt heavy with age. Untouched, like the crypts of an old church, or the hidden cellar beneath a house.

"Okay" – Milo poked his head through a door into a darkened room – "what is up with this place? Where's the fridge, TV, radiators... anything?"

This room centred about a long table with high backed chairs, a chandelier with candles dripping with wax overhead. An iron stove squatted in the corner, with wood piled in a wicker basket next to it.

"Freya," Milo called out, after checking another room, "the corridor doesn't have any windows, right?"

"Yeah, so?"

Milo ignored her tone and said, "If there's no windows and no lights, and the doors to the other rooms are closed, then why is it so easy to see in here? Where is the light coming from?"

She stopped to consider his question. Her crooked nose twitched as she frowned. Milo was right. A peculiar and pervasive light illuminated the rooms, seeping out of the dark wood. Together they leant closer and saw shades of light and dark crawl along the grain of the wood.

"It's moving, Milo. What is this?"

"There has to be a logical explanation." Milo took a long breath, and slowly nodded. "Bioluminescence, bacteria which makes light, growing on the wood."

"Are you sure?"

"I can't think of anything else, can you?"

"Yeah, but I like that bioluminescence thing better."

"You had to say that." Milo closed his eyes. "We stick to science, facts, not horror films."

"Right, let's search this place and then wait outside for James. I have a feeling he'll be here a while – you saw how he was."

There were three small bedrooms each with beds, large for one person. A kitchen, dining room, and a room with a raised back which had a hole – the toilet, they realised. All these rooms had few if any adornments and a couple of paintings so faded it was impossible to make out the details.

"This place is a dump," Milo said.

Freya nodded. They had reached the end of the illuminated corridor. So, the two turned back to the staircase they had seen James and Reg walk down at the front of the house.

"Follow James downstairs or head up?" Milo asked, pushing his glasses up as he peered down the stairs.

Deep shadows moved, though it was empty below, as the constant illumination became brighter and more distorted down the stairs. Light and shadow intertwined, twisting, swaying in patterns which stole across the floor. Locked to a rhythm, to a faint susurration, whisper, of music. A melody sounding at the limits of their consciousness, to inspire a deep unease.

"More bioluminescence?" Freya's voice quivered.

"Yes, I guess... I don't know, Freya," Milo said. "What now?"

Freya looked away from the shadows, mouth twisting, biting her lip. Milo pretended not to see the slight tremor of her hands; he was sure he was worse.

"Upstairs looks fine," Freya said. "Let's explore there."

Milo had started up the stairs before she had even finished speaking. He threw open the large hatch, two doors built straight into the ceiling at the top of the stairs. They swung vertically open and thudded onto the wood of the first floor.

From ground floor to first, from confined to open, and from a dim light to bright. The first floor rose to where beams held the ceiling tiles on high.

Here the curvature of the house was clear. The rear was wide and squared, the front simply a narrow pane of glass. Like swan wings held high and back, from the front window both sides of the wooden walls swept out to rise up and wide in the middle, and curve gently back to the rear.

A cabin encompassed the back quarter of the room. Two flowing staircases led to the floor over the cabin. Fixed over the cabin were solid blocks of wood, to no apparent purpose.

There were two wooden pillars, the tallest rising to form a platform before ascending to the roof. The second pillar stood halfway between the first and the front of the house. Each pillar bore two crossbeams which bisected the room.

Sunlight, warm and dear, poured from that huge, single pane of glass behind them. Dust motes drifted on by, lit by the light; as were the farthest corners of this place, so even the wooden rafters in the far off ceiling made no shadow that was not touched by light.

It was a welcome reprieve, this cavernous, light space which upon entry Freya and Milo did barely stir. They stood side by side, scarcely daring to breathe.

"This place is weird," Milo said, and all Freya could do was nod.

Stillness is a momentary thing, and their curiosity was powerful. So, in slow and quiet steps they began to explore.

While Freya wandered to the back, Milo's attention was captured by the telescope placed under the window. Milo walked into the light under the plane of glass to examine it. Bronze with silver inscriptions, the telescope pointed through the window to where the moon was visible in the late afternoon sky.

Milo looked through the eyepiece.

And saw the world enriched in vast silver-blue currents. The moon came into focus, as an oasis of calm in a surging torrent of that ethereal light. The light flowed in waves around the moon's sanctuary, and vast eddies swirled after the currents left the moon's embrace. The currents of silver-blue ended with the window's edge.

"Damn."

Milo pulled his eyes away from the view and examined the telescope. Over the length of the dust covered bronze, faint silver inlays hid. Brushing the dust away, he was surprised to see the metal bright and untarnished with age. And the silver, the silver was tinged with blue.

Milo gazed through the window, small besides that monolithic plane of glass. The moon was distant and bare now, faded in the blue sky; most certainly without vast currents flowing past it as water does to a pebble.

Milo itched to look through the telescope again. For he felt he now stood upon the cliff of what was known, and whilst staring to the horizon had seen that horizon flutter as though it was a curtain, and not real at all. All he would have to do to look past that horizon curtain, was to look through the telescope once more.

"Milo," Freya said, "let's go. We've seen this bit, let's wait outside for James."

"Outside?" Milo looked back to where Freya was descending the steps leading over the cabin.

"Yeah." Milo looked back at the telescope and shivered. "Yeah, let's go."

...

Freya straightened, the tension in her body easing as she left the house and they walked onto the road. Leaning her head back, she took a long breath. Even London's muggy flavour beat the dust-laden air of the house.

A piercing whistle cut the air. A man in black clothes and a deep hood had one hand to his mouth. The other was drawing a long knife. He stopped whistling and lowered his hand

"You two kids just walked out of that house." The man spat to one side. "You need to come with me."

"What? No, we don't." Freya said.

"Girl, that wasn't a question." The man crossed the street, and the knife gleamed in his hand.

Milo and Freya backed up until their backs pressed against the metal gate of 66 Crescent Way. The man loomed over them, a dark figure before them as he reached to grab Freya's shoulder.

Both Milo and Freya had frozen, but as the man's hand came closer, instincts drilled into Freya by her father came to life. And she kicked the man, with all her strength, right between his legs.

The man whimpered and staggered back. Milo gaped as Freya grabbed and twisted his wrist. He gasped in pain, dropping the knife. He swung with his free hand. She ducked and stepped in close, whipping her elbow smack across his face. He crumpled to the ground.

Enraged cries erupted from one end of the terraced street. Men raced down the tarmac, dressed in the similar dark clothes as the man lying near them. One, a giant of a man, led the pack.

They froze, gripped by a mixture of fear and utter disbelief. '*Move!*' Freya's dad's voice yelled in her mind. '*Freeze and you lose.*'

"Come on!" Freya shook Milo. "We have to get back in the house."

A slim figure emerged from behind the pack of men, a porcelain mask covering her face. Long, black hair hung in waves down her back, and she wore an open, dark coat with large gold buttons and silver trimmings that trailed down past her knees. A loose, white shirt with a frill down the chest was tucked into dark trousers held by a wide belt with a gleaming buckle.

She raised a bow and drew back an arrow which gathered a bright ethereal light and released. It arced up, to shine against the dark clouds. As it fell, the slim figure clenched her raised fist. The arrow exploded, its light warping into a net ready to engulf Freya and Milo.

Freya tackled Milo to the ground, then crouched to hold the net off him so Milo might escape after. Yet the net stilled, held in mid-air. If Freya stretched her hand, she would touch that 'rope' of ethereal light.

"Lass," a kind and old voice said behind her, "best not to touch that."

Freya turned to see an old man holding a gnarled staff aloft. The staff's creases and crevices held the same ethereal light of the net above. The old man waved the staff, and the net above was set gently down to one side.

The pack of men halted behind the giant's outstretched arms. He eyed the old man as one might a lion. The slim figure released her fist and the net dissipated. She strode down the road, bow in hand.

As Freya helped Milo up, the old man turned so he might keep an eye on the men, whilst talking to them. "Is James in the house?"

Freya nodded.

"Good." The old man's smile, despite its warmth, did little to reassure, for men prowled but a little distance away. "I understand that this is confusing but follow my lead and I'll see you safe. Will you trust me?"

"I..." Freya licked her lips and looked at Milo who looked back in equal loss. "I have a question."

"Quickly."

"What's your name?"

"Giles." He smiled, understanding why she would ask. "You must be Freya and Milo. James spoke of you. Will you trust me?"

"Yeah," Freya said, and Milo nodded, too.

"We'll trust you, Giles."

...

"Let's split up. I'll see what Reg is up to, you guys search the rest of the house," James called back, with a rising sense of anticipation.

James reached the stairs at the end of the hall. He knelt and scratched Reg behind the ears. "Where to now, buddy?"

Reg paused for a moment to enjoy the attention. He shook off James's hand and started down the stairs. James was halfway down before he noticed the bizarre light display coming from the bottom floor.

But the basement beckoned, and he answered. The warmth he felt outside grew, fed by the faint susurration, the whisper of music. As he descended, the music rang louder, light and shadow quickening their slow dance. By his side, Reg kept pace and together they touched down on the basement floor.

Light rippled from where his foot and Reg's paw met the floor. A new pattern, the first in an age according to this dust-ridden room. The music advanced, and all James heard were lilting notes soaring high and a quiet thumping dance.

James walked to the beat which itself moved to the time of the lights' display. Each step created a wave, giving the light a new energy, and the music sang louder.

A moth to the flame, as James walked, each new step led to a new wave, a new sound.

James walked the long and wide room with a ceiling just higher than his head. There were many crates and barrels, most made from that same dark wood. Others which weren't lay rotten with age and shards of rusted metal littered the floor. James paid this no heed, instead gliding through the chaos, sure to never miss the beat.

While James's speed never changed, Reg's always did. Reg revolved around James, circling out till he touched the edges of the wall. In a counter play to James, Reg's paws, without a single flaw, fell with the lilting notes.

This display inspired no fear in James, though well it should. Agent of this new design, should he fail, there would be consequences. James knew that he had walked into a lock, and that his steps, and Reg's, were the key. But, with a mind trapped by design, he knew their steps to be right. That this was a lock meant for them and no other.

James and Reg reached the end together and gazed with blank eyes at the wall. As if pulled by a tether, James raised a hand. On command the lights and music froze. A door appeared, shimmering and grand.

His mind came back to himself. He had walked the room, the key had found the lock and turned cleanly. But now he and Reg had opened the lock, he could always walk away.

"No." James laughed at the thought. "That does not sound like me."

James grasped the handle, twisted, and pulled.

The lights once more danced, and with great emotion the music sang its final token. The door was open and now events were firmly set into motion.

James walked through and was captivated.

For rotating in the centre of the room was the Milky Way, a perfect representation of our galaxy.

A radiant sheath of stars whirled around the black hole nestled at the centre of our galaxy. Further out lay its spiral arms, curving out from the bright centre in the way the long dress of a ballerina curves as she spins.

"What kind of house is this...?" James whispered, afraid that to speak any louder would cause this miracle to vanish.

The light of the spiral arms varied along its length. As James moved closer, vivid colours shone as individual features became clear.

He saw clouds of every colour, shining like jewels along the chains of stars. *Nebulae,* he remembered, *they're called nebulae.* Most were in the spiral arms of the galaxy, sculpted by timeless forces.

Enthralled, a bright flash on the next arm caused him to jump. After trying to scrub the spot of light from his vision, James investigated. He ducked underneath the bottom of a large cluster of stars.

He found the source, a small and expanding pearl of vibrant blues and greens. Along the pearl's edge red swaths formed and dissipated, vortexes of energy swirling in and out of existence. James watched until the supernova lost its energy and became another nebula, another jewel encrusted upon the arm of the galaxy.

"Where's Earth on this?" He spoke in awe, numbly giving voice to his thoughts. James was slow to notice a blinking light from the other side of the galaxy. It came from a star about three-quarters out from the centre.

James walked over and touched the blinking star.

It stopped flashing, and James froze. A few moments later, he relaxed and chuckled. Then the display changed.

It focused on the star, the rest of the galaxy disappearing into the walls as the display zoomed in.

James watched, head spinning at the vertigo inducing sight as objects moving past him grew in size and detail. For a split second, his head was engulfed in an expanding nebula cloud. The migraine it caused demanded he close his eyes, despite the spectacle.

His pounding head subsided after a few minutes, and James dared to open his eyes. His breath caught again.

The Sun bathed the room in a warm and orange light, dominating the centre by sheer size. Currents of energy writhed across its surface. Shifting shades of orange and yellow merged and split in a riotous splendour. In the star's ever-changing landscape, mountains were created and dissipated in an instant, and gouts of fire erupted from the darkest patches.

Our eight planets of the solar system circled the Sun, dwarfed in comparison, competing for attention. James saw something out of the corner of his eye. He ducked, looked up and gaped. Saturn passed overhead, its rings radiant.

James shuffled forward. He witnessed Jupiter's march across space. Its numerous moons scurried around it as courtiers attending to their king.

Onwards, to the asteroids in orbit and rarely did they collide. Instead, as each asteroid moved at its own pace, its influence on the others, and theirs on it, waxed and waned. And so, each asteroid danced to the pull of its passing partners, to the changing tune of gravity's touch.

Far smaller than the previous others so far, was Mars the red planet. Its two, tiny, potato-shaped moons kept their distance. White balding patches of ice clung to Mars's poles. Otherwise, its sole defining features was a vast canyon and a colossal mountain.

James cocked his head to one side. *That mountain looks kind of like a pimple just waiting to be popped*, he thought.

Earth swung into view.

It gleamed with the light reflecting off vast tracts of oceans and ice. Its land was a patchwork: the greens of the trees and grass, the yellow of sand and the dull grey of mountains. The influence of humans, of us, could be seen, too, the soft glow and smog of cities and roads forming a web across much of the surface.

The moon circled in its long vigil, a watcher of the dramas of Earth.

Earth continued its orbit and James began to trot to keep up, not yet finished with his examination of his home. "I wish this would stop." At the word stop, the image froze.

"Huh." Halting under Earth, he tilted his head up to inspect it when a thought occurred to him.

"Down?" The image sank down, stopping at his chest height.

"Thanks?" He glanced around and shivered.

James walked around Earth. Light flashed as a huge thunderstorm staked its claim over a portion of the Pacific Ocean. Running like a spine down the Americas the jagged peaks of the Andes and Rockies pierced the clouds.

He looked for Britain, trying to find where his own house would be. He frowned, seeing another blinking light, this time over London. Reaching out he hesitated, remembering what happened last time.

A crooked smile formed. "What's the worst that could happen?"

Yet it was with a trembling hand he touched the light. Nothing happened, as he waited. Slight vibrations shivered up and down the house. A snap, a crack as sharp as glacial ice breaking as spring wakes from winter, and 66 Crescent Way leapt. Whilst being thrown to the floor, James was...

...transported. To every plank of wood, every room, every nail. He felt his weight pressed down on the floor as the floor would feel it. He knew with a sudden certainty that Freya and Milo had left the house.

Emotions, not his own, washed over him. Freedom and an elation so fierce and deep, tears sprang unbidden to his eyes. The elation remained, birthing a determination, a purpose from which it would not be swayed.

So strong was this sense of purpose, so complete, that James found himself urging it on. It recognised his presence, the alien thoughts pausing and focusing on him. It sent a wave of emotions: *Hello*. Then with a sense of gratitude, pushed his focus to the top floor and to the window it held.

It urged him to look out and he saw Freya and Milo with Giles. The view swung to the side, and he saw the press of men and the giant from the night before. A figure dressed in black and holding a bow, walked into sight and the men parted before her. Her features were concealed behind a porcelain mask.

Though he had no hands in this state, he tried to press them against the window. The figure's red painted porcelain lips pressed together, moving as though they were real lips. She, for in daylight it was clear that the figure was a she, frowned. Porcelain moved like a second skin yet when stilled retained its natural hardness.

Curtains along the street were drawn back. An increasing number of eyes were witness to the drama on the street.

She gave a curt command, and her men began to walk away. She looked towards the house. James felt his eyes meet hers, though he was but a spirit watching on. Behind the porcelain mask beautiful, brown eyes widened. She, with black hair flowing down her back, left the scene that he could see.

James opened his eyes, the wooden floor hard beneath him. He tried to stand but tumbled back to the ground, unconscious.

Chapter 6: A Question, and an Argument

"Tea?"

James woke to see Giles's hand pull away from his face. "What?"

"Tea." Giles pulled back to sit by a table, pipe between clenched teeth puffing away, and the galaxy spinning behind him. "Would you like some, lad?"

James shoved off the floor and onto his feet, away from Giles and the spinning galaxy. His limbs rebelled though, stiff as though rested for far too long. James stumbled and fell, only to be caught, drifting down through a cloud of blue-silver, ethereal light.

"After projecting your spirit from your body, it's best to rest a while." Giles had his hand outstretched towards James. As Giles lowered his hand the cloud supporting James lowered, too, till James was sat upon the floor so that his back could rest against the wall.

"Take a second, lad." Giles poured the cup. "Centre yourself. Let your eyes rest on the Star Map there."

Centre yourself? James thought. He lifted a hand to see it trembling. Felt the thrum of each heartbeat, of blood being pumped through distant muscles. The sensation of air filling his lungs, swirling inside them to be pushed back out, the taste of the air, of dust and old wood.

James felt his eyeballs swivel inside his skull as he looked around. He saw the lower halves of Milo and Freya, under the centre of the galaxy, on the other side of its jewelled spiralled arms. Reg leapt into his lap, making him start.

"Hey boy." James stroked his red fur, fingers tingling. "How are you doing?"

Reg nuzzled the crook of James's arm and settled down.

"Here" – Giles approached with the promised cup of tea – "tea helps. I find that is true most of the time."

Giles watched as James took the mug and lifted it to his lips. He sat next to James against the wall.

"I have lived here a long while, but I don't think I have ever sat in this spot and seen this room from here."

"You're sitting there?" James blinked. "Why don't you sit by the table?"

"It would not be proper for me to sit up there while you are here, and you should not move after what you went through. Besides" – Giles gave James a searching glance – "seeing things from new perspectives like that can be difficult."

"I saw you, and Milo, and Freya," James said, a hand flush against the varnished floor and eyes lost to the middle distance. "From the window upstairs, but my body, I was here."

"It's called astral projection when your spirit leaves the body. Even the best feel weak after. For a greenhorn, not having knowledge or experience of ether, you're doing well, lad."

"I am?" James rested his head against the wall and closed his eyes. "My head feels like it was squeezed like, like a pimple as it's being popped. What does doing badly feel like?"

"That..." Giles winced. "Trust me, lad, let's save that for another day."

"That bad?" James asked.

"Aye, that bad."

For a few minutes, they sat there, the room quiet save for the murmured talk of Milo and Freya on the far side of the room.

"Giles?" The old man turned to see James looking at him with pain-filled, pleading eyes. "What the hell is going on? Who are you? How did you catch me then? And that girl in the mask I saw, the one that looked like a pirate, what does she want?"

"Good questions, similar to the ones your friends asked."

"And what did you tell them?"

"That I would wait until you were awake." Giles smiled and called out. "Freya, Milo... James is better now."

The lower halves of Milo and Freya that they could see under the Star Map jumped. James laughed as they ran to him and Giles. Their faces appeared to burst out of the centre of the galaxy as they crossed the large room, footsteps thumping in the quiet.

"James, you're all right," Milo said.

"Look like hell though." Freya squinted down at him and Reg. "That astral projection thing really knocked it out of you, huh?"

"Guess it did, I'm feeling bit better now though."

"So, it really happened?" Milo asked. "You were a ghost?"

"Spirit, a ghost would mean he died, lad. You have questions," Giles said as the friends turned to him, still sitting beside James, "the same that James just asked me. What is going on? You all asked that, word for word."

"Take a seat." Giles nodded to the table. "You're on the edge of it now. Step any further and you'll be right in the thick of it."

"Before I tell you everything, I am going to demand a choice from you. For you are all on a crossroads of your lives. I will not be so cruel, should you choose the safer and perhaps saner path, as to reveal the truth and then leave you bereft of experiencing it ever again."

Freya and Milo sat on chairs beside the table, and James was next to Giles on the wooden floor with Reg in his lap. Though the galaxy spun near them, and all its complex beauty was laid bare, none of the three friends looked anywhere but Giles.

"You three have been thrust into unknown waters. You must understand some context before understanding why this choice is necessary. Namely, why those men are after you."

James, Milo and Freya could not help but lean forwards.

"They are after Reg."

Milo opened his mouth to speak, then stopped and leant back eyes sharp on Giles beneath his glasses.

"Rubbish," Freya said, "I don't believe it!"

"It is the truth, lass."

"Why?" Reg woke and whined as James's voice cracked. "He's just a fox. My fox, my friend. Of all things for them to want, why Reg?"

"Because Reg is not a fox, he is a spirit. A child, you could say, one but recently awoken from a long hibernation. Spirits, especially one like Reg, are incredibly valuable."

Milo jabbed a finger at Giles. "Prove it. Prove it, because I remember Reg peeing in my lap when I was eight years old and that does not seem something like a spirit would do. And I've got plenty more examples like that."

Freya nodded next to Milo, her strawberry curls bouncing.

"He did what?" For the first time, Giles looked surprised. "You want proof Reg is not a fox? The same Reg that does not age, seems to vanish and reappear at will, and is smarter than any fox could be. Is that proof enough?"

James looked to Milo then Giles, then down to Reg and stroked his fine, red fur on his back.

"He doesn't feel like a spirit."

"I know this isn't easy to hear, but those men are here for him, lad. Spirits are valuable to those people cruel enough or ignorant enough to use them for their own ends. Getting one like Reg in the state that he is in now…"

"Well, he is worth more than you can imagine" – Giles shook his head – "and they must not succeed."

Reg shivered and shrank back so James could hold him closer as Giles spoke.

"Stop, you're scaring him."

"James." Giles's voice was gentle. "How could he be scared from words I said, unless what I said is true? No fox could understand human words."

"But he's my…" The words would not come out, and as Reg tried to come closer, James held him tight.

"Is Reg, not Reg?" Freya asked.

"No, lass." Giles commanded their attention. "No, you listen very carefully to what I am about to say, all of you. What he is has changed, who he is has not.

"Your memories of him are true. He is your friend. The friend you've had for as long as you, or he" – Giles looked at Reg and smiled – "can remember."

"Right," Milo said, "that makes sense. He is still Reg."

As Milo spoke those words, James nodded, too. The grip he had on Reg relaxed.

"Hold to that knowledge, lad," Giles said. "Aye, look at the time. Sun's fading, and that means troubles' tide is rising. As I see it, there are three paths before you. I'll tell them to you now, give you the night to think, and for you to come back on the 'morrow."

Giles sat back and took a long drag of his pipe, then he spoke. "First, is the safest and perhaps sanest of the three. Tomorrow, having decided you want no more of this danger, you will come back here give Reg to me and you will never see us again."

"Are you mad?" Freya leapt from her seat, "we're not leaving Reg with you!"

Milo was right beside her. "Yeah, try it, and, and I call the police!"

They turned to James, who glared at Giles and said. "No, where Reg goes, I go."

Giles looked at the three friends arrayed against him, children barely turned teenagers and smiled.

"Though I would have thought less of you if you had said otherwise and abandoned Reg, a part of me wishes you had taken the safer course."

The friends paused and Giles sighed and with aid from his staff he stood. "Let us all move to the table. Milo,

Freya if you could help James up while I pour you a tea."

Only after a good time later, when each of the friends had some tea that warmed them as it went down, and were seated comfortably, with Reg in James lap, around the wooden table did Giles begin again.

"The second choice, and likely most tempting, you try to return to life as normal, or hide with Reg. These men, and their leader will not let that happen. From your last meeting with them it should be clear that they will do anything to capture him. You cannot imagine the distances they have travelled to come here."

James looked to the Star Map, as Giles had called the spinning galaxy, and shivered. Milo and Freya followed his gaze, towards the spinning galaxy, the endless ocean of stars. Their words stilled on their tongues.

"That's not much of a choice either," James said, eventually. "What is the third option?"

"You accompany Reg on his journey, into the unknown. To where he would finally be safe, and free of fear."

Giles's eyes were lit by a strange light that sent the hairs on the back of James's neck to rise and skin to shiver.

"You will embark on a journey of many months, even years. An adventure, James, to places in which Reg will in truth need you."

"You want us to go an adventure with you?" Freya scoffed. "Are you crazy?"

"It is your choice to come or not, but Reg cannot stay. If you choose not to come, he and I must go alone."

"No," James slammed a fist on the table, "Not that, anything but that."

Milo frowned and pushed back his glasses. "Why can't Reg stay here with us, we'll hide. You could help protect him, too, you helped earlier."

"They will find him, as they did before, and I cannot fight all of them. On the 'morrow, come to me with your decision. Whatever it is, I will aid as best I can. But for now, the night is truly falling, and it is best you go home."

They talk a while after that, but Giles refused any more information no matter how much they pressed him. Tomorrow, he said, you have all you need for now.

They walked through the house out into the yard in silence. At the gate at 66 Crescent Way, James turned. "If what you said is right, they're not going to stop."

"No lad, they won't."

"So, what comes next? You've got a plan, haven't you?"

"Aye, I have a plan. But what that plan is will stay with me till you've made your decision."

"This isn't fair, there must be another way."

Milo and Freya turned to face Giles too, and, by the look on their faces, they echoed James. Giles leant on his staff as he looked at the three young friends.

"I'm sorry, I can't see it lad, that another way. We don't decide the choices we face; all we can do is make the best decision we can."

With that, Giles turned around and walked back to the house of 66 Crescent Way, gnarled staff clicking against the concrete stepping-stones.

...

"There's got to be another way," James announced, rising from the sofa.

"James," Milo said, "that's the fifth time you've said that."

They had walked to Milo's house, intent on all three of them staying the night there for safety. All the way back and now curled up on the sofas arranged just past the newly restored Mini in Milo's garage where they had talked, and argued, and talked some more.

"Well, it's true. There must be another way."

"We're not arguing that." Milo leant towards James from where he sat. "I'm just saying, what if there is no other choice, but the ones Giles gave us? What are we going to do then?"

"Sometimes in a fight, you've either got to take a hit in the face or be put in an armbar. And lose the match," Freya explained. "Sometimes, James, you've got two bad options and you got to pick the one that sucks the least."

"I don't accept that."

"Fine." Milo threw up his hands. "Let's talk about the other bit."

"What other bit?"

"That nonsense that Reg is not a fox, but a spirit."

"I was trying not to think about that," James said. "I don't want him to be. I don't want this to change."

"Well, Freya are you are buying it?"

"Yeah." Freya stroked Reg's fur as she spoke. "We all knew there was something off about Reg anyway."

James stirred as Reg barked and batted at Freya's thigh after she said that.

"Not off in a bad way, Reg, just that you're special."

Reg purred as Freya continued to stroke his fur.

"And that doesn't bother you?"

"No, he's still Reg. Does it bother you?"

"Of course, it does," Milo said. "Am I the only sane one here? How are you taking this so well?"

"Milo," James said, his voice rising, "he's still Reg. He's still the one who tripped Billy when he was chasing you in Year Six."

"I know, James, but…"

"The one who leapt into the pond to get your sinking mechanical boat when we were five." James stabbed his finger towards him.

"James, I know…"

"Reg is our friend, Milo!"

"James," Freya said, "he gets it."

Milo was pressed back against the sofa. James blinked. His throat was hoarse, and he could hear echoes of his last sentence bouncing back to him from the upstairs floor. James lowered his finger.

"Sorry, Milo, I- I need a second outside." James walked around the Mini and out of the room and slammed the door behind him. They heard the front door open, and slam shut.

"Reckon he's all right?" Freya asked.

"No. Don't think I'm all right either. Why did he have to go and say that?"

Milo yanked out a stubborn piece of thread from the old sofa, then drank half of his hot tea and set the mug down with a thud. Freya rolled her eyes, flicked some lint his way and watched blink in surprise behind his thick glasses.

"Because he's worried about Reg, stupid."

"Hey, feelings."

"Sorry. He didn't mean it, Milo."

"I know." And for a few minutes they sat there in silence.

"Are you okay?" Milo asked.

Freya brought Reg up so she could hug him in her arms. "No, we got attacked today, how could I be okay? What do you think is going to happen?"

"I- I don't know…" Milo pushed his glasses back and sighed. "I'm going to check on James."

"Yeah, good idea."

Milo closed the door behind him. Freya lifted Reg up, and said, "I'm not going to let anything happen to you, Reg, I promise."

Reg licked her face.

"Reg, that's gross." Freya laughed, holding Reg away as he tried to lick her again.

"Freya," Milo shouted, footsteps thumping as he ran back in. "Freya, he's gone."

"What?" Freya and Reg both looked at Milo as he burst through the door.

"James, he's not there."

Freya dropped Reg as he began to howl.

Chapter 7: Caught in the Huntress' Snare

James approached Clapham Common.

It had, James noted idly, turned into a nice evening, as there was not a cloud in the sky. The last orange rays were fading, and the moon was full to paint the world in silver tones.

He had not planned this, even after the door had closed behind him. But his feet had taken him forward almost before his mind had the thought to go.

He walked with the same certainty of a raindrop that would eventually hit the ground. Everything looked too normal, the cars driving past, people eating dinner by the window, laughing and talking as though nothing had changed. James scowled, and his pace quickened.

He sprinted past 66 Crescent Way and paused after to look back at the tall and grim house glimpsed behind the thick yew. James shook his head and continued. He did not want to talk to Giles, to hear his wise, kind words. And the vague answers that came with them.

James quickened his stride across the road and skipped past a car which blared its horn at him. The driver yelled out of the open window. Past the bench where he had woken and saw the world wreathed in blue-silver fire. The air alive and awash in ethereal currents. When the had been veil lifted from his eyes and seen a tree crowned in glory.

For a few brief seconds are too short a glimpse of proof of the eternal. Too brief in witnessing the heartbeat of the infinite universe. Too little time to see the beauty that is written of heaven embodied by a single tree.

Yet still James did not believe. He walked to where Giles, Reg and he had been surrounded the night before and saw the small crater Giles had blown into the path with his staff.

Onwards, to where this strangeness that sought to upturn his life, with iron fist knock him out of his natural orbit, had started.

James turned the blind corner around an old, red brick wall wreathed in ivy, surrounding Holy Trinity Church on the common, and stopped.

There she was, wearing her porcelain mask and pirate clothes, with a bow slung across her back and jade bracelet loose on her arm.

"At least you decided not to knock me over this time," James said.

She tilted her head, regarding him.

"Take off that mask."

The porcelain narrowed as her eyes did.

"I know who you are. Take it off."

"Are you sure?" she asked, and her voice made him certain.

"Yeah, take off the mask."

The figure reached up, and gently lifted the mask off her face.

"James," Artemis said, "it was a mistake to come out here by yourself."

"Artemis…"

"No questions, James? Nothing to say?"

"No, too many questions." James looked around at the darkening sky, seeing grey figures standing back at a distance. "But it all comes back to you."

Artemis blinked and pursed her lips. "Why did you come here, James?"

"I want to know what the hell is going on. Ever since I met you, everything has been turned upside down."

"I suppose it would seem like that to you."

"Why? Are you really just here, doing all of this, for Reg?"

Her eyes, so large and beautiful, pierced his own.

"Yes," she said. "Give him to me and this will all be over."

"Are you insane? No, he's my friend."

"Then I will take him," and James realised what it was to be a mouse stared down by a hawk. "Now you are here, you will help me with that whether you want to or not."

"No. Even if you do take him, wherever on Earth you go, I'll follow."

One of the grey figures snorted at that. Artemis glared at the man, and he dipped his head and shuffled back. It was only then, as his outrage and confusion faded, that James realised he was surrounded.

"Search every inch of this planet if you like." Artemis bared teeth in a smile and shook her head. "It won't matter."

"What do you mean by that?"

"Open your eyes, James. This place, your home, is so small, understands so little. I would see you accept what is happening before I take your Reg and leave you behind.

"Tell me" – Artemis stepped forward – "answer your own question. I thought more of you than this."

"The only answer is impossible." James could scarcely breathe, or he was breathing too fast, he did not know.

"Impossible?" She snarled and a rope of blue-silver light was created in the grasp of her hand.

Artemis whipped the rope forward, and it lashed around James's neck. He cried out as it transformed to a noose as the different lines merged into a smooth circle. "Is this rope of ether impossible? Am I impossible?"

"Can you not say it, nor even think it?"

Artemis gestured and her men began to step out of the shadows. The giant of a man held out a tricorn hat for her, and said, "Captain."

Artemis took the hat and placed atop her head. Now she looked as a pirate captain, James's ethereal noose in one hand her crew all around.

"I have heard a phrase in my time here, a question." She said.

"Are we alone in the universe?"

Her men laughed, and this time Artemis did not stop them. "Take a look around, tell me if you can guess the answer. Samael, give him some more light so he can see."

Samael, the giant of a man conjured a ball of blue-silver light, of ether, atop the palm of his hand. The light showed the men in sharp relief, and not all were human.

One with four arms reached up to pull back a deep hood. One eye dominated its head, blue skin stretched tight against bone. Its mouth opened to reveal rows of sharp, pointed teeth. "You are in the deep ether now, boy," it said.

Another with gloves on normal hands pulled its hood back. Light glinted off its metallic face, with features finely wrought. Its eyes sparked with an ethereal light, and the quirk of its lips could only be called a smirk. It clicked its fingers, a sharp, metal snap. A dagger appeared in its palm with which it began to play, to dance it between its fingers. All the while its eyes never left James.

"Darling," it said, each word ringing clear. "Always a pleasure to meet a fellow fool."

Another collapsed and writhed on the ground with much hissing and snapping, which stopped with a sudden screech. Delicately an insect leg, thin like a whip, unfurled from the bottom of the coat. Another leg emerged, and another, and another, and then many, many more, straightening and beginning to drag something out, as it still hissed and snapped in vile frustration.

There were others, oh, there were others, each as hideous or strange to James's human, or Earthen, sensibilities. But those were the only ones who dared speak. The rest looked to Artemis, their self-evident captain, to lead.

"James" – and the ethereal noose tightened around his neck – "when you are hunting elusive prey, you must tighten the cordon, the net, around it until it has no option but to face you rather than run."

The noose yanked James off his feet, though Artemis did not move. A thought was all that was needed to shorten the ethereal rope Artemis held.

"You are what I need to have. For that spirit to face me rather than run."

The pain of falling acted like ice water dumped on his head, and what Artemis said roused him to speak.

"His name is Reg."

James tugged at the noose around his neck. His fingers found no purchase on the ethereal rope.

"Spirits are concentrated ether, no more worthy of empathy than a tree, lake, or flower." Artemis spoke as though quoting something. "Reg is no more alive than the grass you are lying on."

"You've met Reg, you stroked him. That is the stupidest thing I ever heard."

"It doesn't matter what you think. That spirit, your Reg – I could buy this ether-starved planet with what he is worth. He is exactly what I have been looking for."

"This planet?"

"You know nothing," Artemis laughed, and it was not a kind sound. "I wondered what it would be like to live so blissfully ignorant on planets like these. Now I know."

Her men laughed with her but hushed as she spoke. "Spirits can be used to do anything, and I do mean anything, James. One like Reg, half the galaxy will be after him. I do not know what it, Reg, is doing here on this backwater planet. Nor who that old man is. But with you to bargain with? Your Reg is as good as mine."

"This can't be real."

"Real?" The ethereal noose flexed, and James gasped, fingers scrambling at the noose, unable to breathe. "Is that real enough for you, James?"

A howl, high-pitched and keening, split the midnight air. A howl that echoed to shiver your bones and freeze your ethereal soul.

Everyone flinched as though slapped.

"It's here, Samael," Artemis said, and the giant straightened. "Crew, form a line to capture the spirit."

Reg raced across the common. Behind him a car roared, accelerating over the pavement onto the grass. Reg blazed scarlet and a wave of ether gathered in his wake.

Samael leapt in front of Artemis. Her men rushed out in a loose semi-circle to ensnare Reg. Yet Reg shone as a red star against the common's green. They slowed as the wave behind him grew into a cascade of ethereal radiance. He came to challenge Artemis and her crew, a force of nature, young but powerful.

Reg, larger than before, hurtled through the crew as a cannon ball through wicker walls. He lunged at the ethereal rope Artemis held and bit clean through it.

The ethereal wave behind him picked up and tossed the crew aside like flotsam discarded by the tide, thrown against the ground, battered against the trees.

One man soared to crash against the church and, while falling, his clothes were snagged by a stone, leaving him to hang. James was left untouched.

Samael stepped in front of Artemis and thrust out his hands, legs braced for impact. A half cone shimmered into existence around them, its point facing towards the wave. The ether crashed into the cone, and his immense arms bulged. Samael's will was fully realised and concentrated, while the wave held power that was not focused.

Samuel clung to his, and Artemis', defence like a limpet clings to a rock. He endured, while Artemis paid no heed to the wave but looked with hungry eyes to Reg.

Reg shone, a spirit revealed on Clapham Common, illuminating the midnight hour. He howled again, a great fox, bright yet indistinct, standing between James and Artemis.

"Do you see, James? Is the truth clear now?" Artemis cried, arm before her eyes as she pushed against the force of Reg's howl.

"Reg?" James wiped his eyes and still he saw Reg as a ghostly figure swirling ethereal light.

A horn blared, a weak 'puut' of a sound compared to the power that was displayed before, but it was a sound James knew well. James spun as an newly restored Mini slid to a stop metres away.

"James," Milo called from the open car window, "get in!"

Freya kicked the door open as James ran for the car.

"Reg, come on!" James leapt inside and the Mini coughed, then drove. Reg blurred and appeared in James's arms, in his normal size and dimming in colour.

Artemis unhooked her bow and as she took aim said, "Samael, gather the men. They are going back to that house, gather what men are able and follow. Send one back to prepare the rest of the crew to leave immediately."

The arrow gleamed as Artemis loosed it from the bow. An ethereal line trailed from behind the arrow to the bow. The arrow plunged into the back of the Mini, and the line held snapping taut between Artemis and the car. Ether, near frictionless with the ground, pooled beneath Artemis as the line swept her forward.

Artemis surfed on ether across Clapham Common. She had attached the ethereal line from her bow to wrap around her waist. Another ether-filled arrow pulled against her bowstring. It flew at the Mini as Artemis raced through the trees.

Milo swerved to avoid a dip in the green. Light flashed, a boom shuddering the Mini. A smoking crater appeared where the car would have been.

"What was that?" Milo fought to control the car.

"It's Artemis." James stared through the back window. "She's behind us."

"Artemis?" Freya turned back from the front. "Wait, your girlfriend is the one who's been chasing us?"

"She's not my girlfriend."

"Guys" – Milo shoved his glasses back from where they threatened to rattle off his nose – "keep your eyes peeled in case James's girlfriend tries to blow us up again."

"She's not my…"

Freya shoved the steering wheel in Milo's hands. The Mini careened to the left, tilting on two wheels. The arrow exploded, the light blinding and sound deafening. The explosion shoved the car back down. James, with Reg in his arms, and Freya were sent tumbling in the car. Milo was the only one with his seatbelt on.

"Freya, give me more warning next time." Milo threaded the car through the line of trees. The Mini burst into the road and down Crescent Way. Artemis held on, pulling herself closer along the line.

The brakes squealed and the Mini slid to a stop. Artemis snarled, blasting ether out of her feet to flip, spinning, over the car. She landed on a cloud of ether which slowed her fall until she touched the ground softly, an arrow nocked.

The friends, who were halfway out of the car, froze.

"You" – Artemis pointed the bow at Milo – "take your hand out of the bag slowly."

Milo released the BB gun inside the bag and raised his hands. The backpack slumped down to hang off his elbow. Artemis swung the bow back to James.

"Give me the spirit."

"No." James put Reg behind him who slumped, exhausted, against the ground. "Not on my life."

"Yeah." Freya stood by James. "You'll have to get past me."

"And me." Milo, who looked far from convinced of their ability to do anything against Artemis, nonetheless stood by his friends.

"Move, James." Artemis drew back the bowstring.

"No."

An arrow cut a thin line across his cheek. Strands of hair and splashes of blood fell.

"Move." Artemis nocked another arrow and this one was aimed at his chest.

James touched his cheek and saw blood on his fingertips.

It is strange what you notice when you believe that you are about to die. James saw her hands shake and her face express a twist of emotions. Uncomposed, as

James had only seen her once before – when they had first met, and she'd laughed.

James swallowed, the world slowed, and it seemed another spoke the word.

"No."

Artemis loosed the arrow. It flashed forward, and James gasped. An ethereal hand had caught it in mid-air.

"Just in time, lad." The ghostly hand snapped the arrow.

James, half-convinced he was dead, turned to see Giles push open the creaky iron gate of 66 Crescent Way. His other hand outstretched and closed into a fist.

"You're safe now," he said.

"No!" Artemis shot an ether-filled arrow at Giles.

Giles waved his hand, and its ethereal twin slapped the arrow out of the air with a corresponding boom. The ethereal hand leapt forward as Giles thrust forward his own. The palm of that ghostly appendage rested on Artemis's forehead and Giles said:

"Sleep."

Artemis's eyes rolled up in her head, and she fell forward. Until the jade bracelet on her arm flashed. Giles's ethereal hand shattered, and he staggered as though struck. Artemis caught herself against the ground. She leapt back, propelled by ether. An arrow flashed towards Giles, who blocked it with his staff.

Artemis fired three more arrows in quick succession. Giles, staff spinning, knocked each one from the air.

"Who are you, old man?" Artemis pulled the bowstring and arrow back to her cheek. The arrow began to shine brighter than any others before it.

"Get into the house," Giles said, and slammed his staff onto the pavement. The friends ran.

An ethereal wall gathered between Giles and Artemis so thick and concentrated that it seemed more stuff existed in that space than could be possible. It did not shine with the uncontrolled light held in Artemis's arrow. No, it swirled inside as an ever-changing mosaic of translucent blue-silver ether.

Artemis became blurred when seen through the wall, except the arrow which shone ever brighter. She loosed that arrow and it flew as a comet from the bow. The ground shook and her ears rang. Artemis had to shield herself from the light and flying debris.

She peered through the dust, eyes widening. The road and pavement were ruined in front of Giles, a crater torn from solid tarmac. It was not behind the fading wall Giles had conjured, though. No, that looked precisely as it had before. Breath ragged, she tensed seeing the ether of the wall coalesce into a ball over Giles's hand.

Power rested in his palm, held by his will.

So much so that the dust which fell too close to it, fell instead to the ball and not to the Earth and gathered in orbit around it. The ball was clear as crystal, save for its depths where it sparkled with crystalline motes of pure ether.

Were Artemis another person, she would have thrown her bow down and yelled in frustration. Or screamed and run from the power Giles displayed. But for all else that she was, Artemis was neither a fool nor a coward.

"Who are you?"

Giles was indistinct, along with the trees and pavement around him, as all the natural ether of the area gathered to his palm.

"I am Giles, and you are?"

"Artemis, Princess Artemis, daughter to the Pirate Lord of the Eagle Nebula, Ruler of the Pillars of Creation."

"Pirate Lord," Giles chuckled. "Does he have a name, this lord?"

"Lord 'Blackheart' Kai, ruler–" Artemis paused, thinking that she saw the ball wobble for a moment in Giles's palm upon her saying her father's name. "Ruler for a thousand years."

Giles's eye widened, and the ball cracked. Ether scythed out, gouging the road and tearing the Mini in half. Artemis backed away as Giles held the ball high. His silver hair and old sailor's clothes were pulled by the wind of the ethereal ball as it began to spin, threatening to burst. It bulged to three times its size and Giles's face twisted with pained concentration.

His other hand swept up and plucked at the ball.

Streams of ether leapt from the ball to the yew trees surrounding the house. It sank into the dense and green needle leaves of the yew. Each tree grew, fattened, and swelled. The yew trees which had seemed a somewhat extreme measure for privacy fast became a living wall. Giles walked through the open gate and past the closing gap between the growing trees.

Artemis raced forward, seeing him leave and a barrier soon erected. Giles, without looking back, plucked a new stream from the dwindling ball and threw it back. It engulfed Artemis, tossing her aside. She tumbled through the air, sent sprawling on the tarmac.

Giles then grasped that stream at its base of the ball and redirected it to the yew trees. He left the ball hanging in the air as he walked to the house. It hung between the trees, to be swallowed by the yew whose growth it fed.

The yew stopped, no trace of the house behind the now impenetrable yew needles. Artemis, though it pained her after her own extensive manipulation of ether, fired another charged shot into the now massive yew. Green needles flew in the air, a hole blasted into a tree.

She saw a dark tangle of branches before the needles grew back as before. An abundance of ether still lingered in these trees yet.

Artemis slung her bow across her back and waited for her crew. She did not have the power to break this barrier alone.

Chapter 8: Star Ascending

Giles heard timid knocking above. James, Freya, Milo, and Reg were safe and sound behind the window on the first floor. They looked down on him with wide eyes as James let his hand drop back down.

"Never rains but it pours." Giles turned to look at the wall of yew and sighed. "I let that get away from me."

He pulled out his pipe, set it between his teeth and lit it with a snap of his fingers. "Never too old to be a fool. But the die has been cast and they are safe yet."

Giles walked around the side of the house and into the door, staff tapping and pipe smoking. Down the narrow corridor, his steps were faster and louder than they had been for a long time. A slight smile had grown by the corridor's end despite the difficulty of what he must ask them to do again. For the die was cast, and after so long waiting it was finally time.

On the staircase he laid his hand on the railing and felt it tremble, too. "Aye, my lady, this is it. I can feel it in my bones."

He walked up and out of the hatch to where the friends waited.

"What was that out there?" James asked.

"A safeguard, lad. Those trees need only to hold for a little while."

"Do you never give straight answers?" Freya said.

"I don't want to be giving the wrong ideas, lass, that's all. By the time you get to my age, life's taught you a bit about caution." Giles exhaled a plume of smoke. "Now since you came with trouble knocking on my door, I have a couple of questions for you. Tell me how you came to such trouble in the short time since I last saw you."

James told the story, and Milo and Freya interjected in parts but mostly listened. They were also curious, too.

"James, lad," Giles said afterwards, "it was a brave act to seek out the enemy for answers, when you could debate between friends instead. To try carve a fourth choice out of the three you had."

"Stupid act," Freya said.

"Aye, it could be called that, too."

"It worked though, I know what to do now," James said.

"Good you have an answer, if obtained at great risk. Stars and ether, I thought the last captain was bad."

"The last what?" Milo asked, hoisting his backpack higher up his shoulders.

"Sharp, but one more question first." Giles pointed the end of his pipe towards James. "The choice I asked earlier today, I'll ask it to you again, lad. Are you ready for an adventure?"

James shook his head and glanced at Reg. Blinked, then swung back sharply to Giles and took a long breath.

"Reg and I, we'll go with you on your adventure. We must. Artemis won't stop."

"James," Freya started, "are you sure?"

"You heard the story, Freya. Reg is a one-fox goldrush — we have to go."

"James" — Milo folded his arms — "what about our families though?"

"My parents are safe here, and Reg is family, too." James frowned. "You protect the ones in danger, right, and… Wait, you said 'our families'. You can't come with us. You guys could die."

"That's not for you to say, James." Milo shoved his glasses back. "That's not your decision. It's mine, and Freya's."

"Guys, your families are here."

"Yeah." Freya stamped a foot down. "You and Reg are family, too, idiot."

Milo nodded to that, especially when Freya called James an idiot.

"Guys…"

"You're the idiot brother I never wanted." Freya punched James on the shoulder. "I haven't forgotten that you nearly got yourself captured tonight just to get some answers from your girlfriend."

"She's not my girlfriend." James rubbed his shoulder and winced. "And it did work. I got answers and got out."

"Because we were there," Milo said. "That's the point, isn't it? Like you said, our families are safe here. You, you will get yourself killed without us, James, and Reg captured. I'm going."

"Me, too," Freya said.

"Giles." James looked helpless. "Any help?"

"Lad, from what I heard tonight, you need them. Like Reg needs you."

James looked away from them all, threw up his hands and walked back to stare out the great window to the yew hedge and star-filled sky.

Milo walked over and placed a hand on his shoulder. "You're not winning this one, James, we're coming."

"Thought I was the stubborn one."

"You are," Freya said, and punched his shoulder again.

"Freya" – James rolled his shoulder forward – "cut it out."

"Nope, going to keep doing that for as long as you were stupid today."

"...Great."

"You folks made up your mind to come then?" They turned back to where Giles waited with a smile.

"Yeah," James said, "guess we're all coming."

"Didn't doubt it for a second, lad." Giles puffed on his pipe, his back straighter now and his head held high. A touch of something greater than the elder sailor they knew had fallen over Giles again; something old and weathered, and not yet forgotten.

"Aye, nary a cloud in the sky and the Aetherium beckons. Come."

Giles spun on his heel and marched up the stairs, to the roof of the cabin which sat at the back of the vast first floor. The friends rushed to keep up.

What awaited them was a semi-circular block of wood, wide and as tall as Giles's chest. Behind the railing one could observe the quiet of this strange place. The two great pillars stretched from floor to ceiling, each bearing two crossbeams, and, at the front of the house, in the window that spanned from the floor to roof the moon was bright. Such space and odd design that they could not fathom its purpose.

"Giles," James asked, "what are we doing now?"

"Now, lad, the adventure begins."

"Now?" Milo glanced around. "No time to prepare?"

"Time, time has been a'waiting, too long waiting." Giles began to lift the gnarled staff, stopped, and gave a wry smile.

"Here, lad." Giles held out the staff to James. "It should be you, not I."

"Me?" James said but took the offered staff.

James felt a hum of energy in the wood under his hand and experienced a warmth around him. A presence enveloped him as it had once before in this house – the same strange presence as when his spirit had left his body. Together, he and this presence touched the staff upon the wood before him.

Ether bloomed, unfolding like the way a flower opens its petals, from where the staff touched. Gentle and vast, something awoke fully, and stretched. Ether in blue-silver currents swirled, so that their hair and clothes were loose and lifted. Giles wiped tears from his wrinkled face, and his old eyes gleamed with new life. Milo and Freya backed away, and each drew closer to the other.

James, with Reg upon his shoulders, held the staff against the wood, which moved beneath it as though alive. The semi-circular block of wood transformed to a wooden wheel, so large that James would have to turn it with both hands. Two pillars, one on either side of him, now held levers that he could easily reach. James grasped the wheel, letting the staff drop.

The house shook, as sharp cracks echoed from its foundations. The friends were thrown from their feet.

"Giles!" Freya scrambled back up. "What's happening?"

"Lass, I'd grab the railing as Milo is." Giles used the ether to pick his staff up again. "Hold on tight, there's nothing to do now but bear witness."

Freya tumbled down as the house shook again. She crawled to where Milo hung onto the railing for dear life. Milo grabbed her hand and pulled her close.

"Look" – Milo's voice was faint, and his hand trembled as he pointed up – "the ceiling."

Blood drained from Freya's face. Cracks splintered the wooden ceiling, till it looked so fragile that a feather's weight might be too much. Long lattices of ropes fell from the walls, connecting the floor to the two pillars. The cracks spread to all four walls, and down to the floor, in a web that threatened to burst, to let the outside in and make a mockery of the unconscious safety that walls bring.

James saw Milo's hand and looked up. "Holy..."

The ether surged to fling the fractured wood away. With gunshot snaps, and wooden cracks, the ceiling and walls were there no more. Fragments flung high into the night sky, and were replaced by the fresh scent of yew, by stars and the moon on high.

Only a stout railing remained around the perimeter of the floor. The back of the house had fallen away, but at the front the thick window frame and glass melted and merged into a small, shining pillar. This hung out of the front at a low angle, so its tip rested high on the yew. Underneath it could be glimpsed a statue of a woman, wrought of pure glass.

The cracks and splintering echoed into the distance and the shaking halted. A veneer of peace and quiet descended. Ether drifted back into the wood, gently brought back by unseen hands, and gathered from the yew as well which began to shrink back down.

Milo and Freya stood, and James unclenched his hands from the wheel though he still held it. They gazed up at the stars, through space where there used to be walls.

Ethereal light formed on the wooden floor like a second skin. The friends failed to notice as the light solidified, obscuring the wood beneath it.

Milo squinted upwards. "Those ropes with the pillars and crossbeams, don't they look like…"

The house wrenched itself upwards, sending them sprawling into the floor. It hovered for an instant, then fell back down to Earth and the friends followed.

"This isn't happening." Freya lurched to hug the railing again. "This isn't happening…"

Dazed, Milo managed to stand. A hand crept up to touch blood streaming from a cut on his scalp, his eyes wide and panicked.

James groaned, winded, unable to breathe. The light had risen as the house had jumped. The house rose, they screamed, it again fell to the ground. Faces flat on the floor, none of them could fail to notice the rising light.

"What the..." Freya said.

"Why, what?" Milo's mind rejected what his eyes continued to send. "James, what did you do?"

James remembered the map of the galaxy in the basement and saw the two pillars which rose as masts from the floor.

"Guys." He swallowed, and grimaced. Bile burned his throat. "I don't think this is a hous–"

Another massive wrench and James, Milo and Freya were flattened against the floor. Like a dog yanking on its leash, the structure began to jump higher and higher. Each time, the layer of ethereal light rose.

Panicked yelps from Reg, helpless and bouncing towards the railing, was too light to stop. James scrambled over the buckling floor and leapt. He caught Reg, leaning out over the railing. With one arm, he cradled Reg to his chest as he turned and slid to the floor. His other hand clamped to the railing.

James's world reeled upwards. As he fell back down, he heard a thud. An arrow vibrated in the railing, inches away from where he clung. He looked to see where it had come from. Artemis glared up at him, surrounded by her battered crew.

The threat in her gaze jolted a part of James awake. For reasons afterwards he could never quite remember, James tugged the arrow out of the wood and gave Artemis a grin. He waved it at her and scrambled back to the wheel, just in case she decided to fire another.

Reg held tight, enduring the bruising and battering as James fought his way back to cling to the wheel.

"James!" Milo yelled as the house leapt up. James's stomach turned as they fell back down.

James saw that Milo and Freya had made their way to the other side of the wheel, which they clung to for all they were worth.

"Is Reg okay?" Milo asked, and James nodded.

The house, quivering with the effort, lifted itself ever higher before dropping back down.

"Look up at the beams!" Freya winced as the house crashed down again.

"Beams?"

James looked up, muscles trembling from the pounding he'd received, and again was rendered speechless. The light had jumped past the two large crossbeams, one on each pillar, and now they glowed with a peculiar intensity.

Crossbeams unfurled, losing volume as black sheets unravelled from them. Sheets were pulled down by two ropes at both lower corners. The sheets were pushed taut and strained against the ropes despite this windless night.

James watched as the truth revealed itself. A smaller set of sails unfurled between the upper crossbeams as the ethereal light jumped past them, too. At the front, over the low-hanging pillar and suspended by ropes, a smaller sheet formed a long triangle.

Not believing but with eyes still seeing what was now plain and clear, James realised that the house was, in fact, a ship.

A shroud of light now lay over the entire structure, over the ship. Through the shroud, past trees and in the sane world of terraced houses, of roads and cars, lights were being turned on and curtains thrown back. People walked out, dumbstruck as the house they had mocked, now tried to escape the street which held it in such low regard.

The ship flung itself up through the trees and out over the road. Freya and Milo screamed, sure that it would fall back down. Artemis and her crew scattering beneath them. Yet an energy filled James. It rushed up from the deck and wiped away his fear, to be replaced by a soaring confidence.

For a second, the ship looked to fall, as it had so many times before.

"Now," James said.

The energy rushed out of him. The light of the shroud sped back into the ship and caused it to shine with a ghostly radiance. Sails strained outwards and the ship flew.

And to the people who watched from the street, it looked as a star, ascending to the heavens to join its kin.

Chapter 9: The Fury Rose

James sat at the prow of the ship, Reg by his feet and felt the ethereal wind brush against his face. Space, its tapestry of stars, was immense before him. The Earth and moon were two orbs, diminishing behind the ship.

The house, the ship had flown. The friends had watched London fall away. Saw cars then houses shrink and become a coloured blur. The yellow web of roads merged into a constant glow. London's commons, its parks, were a dark patchwork and the Thames split the city in a dark and winding line.

The ship had swerved, its masts skimming the bottom of a low cloud. Milo fainted at that, as Freya began to shake. James had numbly followed Giles's instructions. His arms felt distant from his body as he picked up Milo's legs, and Giles his torso with ether. Giles kept the ether under Milo as he helped Freya down the stairs. Reg stayed behind.

They had walked down the stairs and through the hatch, which closed itself behind them. Into the dining room, where they had placed Milo onto the long table.

James and Freya had sat shivering in chairs. Giles prepared three mugs of spiced apple tea and set the kettle to boil. Then Giles placed his palm over Milo's forehead.

"He is okay. I could wake him," Giles said, as the kettle quickly boiled, "but better he has a natural rest."

Giles had poured the boiling water into the mugs, and the room had filled with the scent of cinnamon, honey, and apple.

"Try some." Giles placed the mugs before them, with some bread and cheese as well.

As they sipped the spiced apple tea, he said, "I am going to put Milo on a bed. Then, I think, it is best if you eat what you can and do the same."

Freya had bit into the bread and cheese and grimaced before swallowing.

"I think I'm going to lie down for a second," she said.

"Aye," Giles said. "Lad?"

"What?" James looked up from his mug. "Yeah, I'll do the same."

"Follow me then."

Giles had gently lifted Milo up upon a cloud of ether. He directed Milo out of the room and Freya followed, holding the warm cup of tea in both hands. James followed then paused to get Milo's mug, too. Through the door, he saw that Milo was resting on a bed and placed the tea next to him. He walked behind Giles as Freya was shown to her room.

"Captain, lad," Giles said, "this way."

Down the corridor and up the steps, and the hatch opened by itself before them.

"Quickly, best just to get you in your cabin, lad."

The ship was breaking the atmosphere. Earth curved under them, and the stars and Sun were so bright. James had let Giles guide him into the cabin under the helm, but not for one second could he look away. So, he did not notice Reg follow them either.

He sat on the bed, tea in his hands as Giles told him to rest and that he had to check on Milo. The door opened and gently clicked shut. James breathed and sipped the tea. *Kerrrach.* James looked up. Reg was scratching the door, a pair of wood-carved goggles held in his mouth.

"Reg," but James remembered what he had seen all too briefly as he had crossed the deck. *Keeeerrrrrrach,* and Reg pointed to the door with a paw.

"Really?" James asked.

"Woof," Reg barked back.

James walked over, leaving the tea by the bedside table, and knelt before Reg. "You sure, buddy?"

Reg dipped his red furred head down and up.

"Okay." A crooked smile found its way to James's face. He opened the door.

Stars blazed against an endless void. The moon, surface littered by craters, was larger than he had ever seen. The Sun was a white orb, hanging just left of the Earth behind the ship. He saw night-time over Britain, and dawn move across China as the Earth rotated.

And though James did not know it, the ethereal shroud around the ship stopped too much sunlight from entering and blinding him.

James stood there, not feeling the tears running down his cheek, nor the open-mouthed smile that formed. He walked forward, constantly turning his head, until he stood at the prow of the ship, arms braced against the railing.

Slowly he sat, Reg by his feet, head resting between two pillars of the railing. Space stretched before him, and they sailed towards a tapestry of stars.

Something gleaned beneath him, under the bowsprit, the jutting pillar of wood that pierced the space before the ship. The figurehead of this ship that he had glimpsed before. She, the figurehead, was wrought of glass, head thrown back and clothed in wind swept robes. She pointed forward, daring whomever venture with her to venture ever on into the cosmos.

Reg nudged him and dumped the goggles in his mouth at James's feet. After wiping the goggles clean of fox spit, James put them on and the Aetherium appeared.

It was as he saw on the common, where he perceived a tree crowned in glory. Yet here James felt as an ant trying to comprehend a mountain, such was the ocean of ether before him, and yet even this was but the tiniest part of the Aetherium. Ethereal waves pulsed through our solar system, in which all our heavenly bodies, our Sun and planets, were as driftwood bobbing on the tide.

Reg bumped his leg and James saw him in the Aetherium. All else was stained in blue-silver, but Reg was radiant in red and gold. This light washed off him in smoky streams to pool and dissipate from the deck.

"Whoa, hey buddy." James stroked Reg, seeing a puff of his light each time he did so. "I guess you really are a spirit. Still hard to believe…"

James shivered, stepped back and bumped into the side of the telescope at the prow. He took off the goggles, letting them hang around his neck. The telescope gleamed as though newly polished, and one of the silver inscribed symbols on its side glowed. James looked through it and saw the Aetherium again. He pressed the glowing symbol and the ether he saw faded. Other symbols zoomed the telescope's sight in and out, to drizzling degrees.

James scoured the Aetherium with the telescope. Each object he saw was a marvel he vowed to show Milo and Freya.

After a long while, he grew accustomed to the sight and began to think. Of the map in the hold below and the pinpricks of light, each one a star. He looked to the ship's billowing sails, pushed by ether, and again he smiled as he leant over the railing and saw the curve of the ship and stars below. The ship's graceful symmetry caught his gaze as the dark wood curved out and down on either side.

James walked the ship's perimeter, hand running over the railing, and took in every detail: the two masts, a crow's nest, the gleam on the sails, thick ropes which hung everywhere, the worn and dark deck, the bowsprit of glass and dark wood jutting forward.

His smile grew.

Up the stairs, over the cabin that was now his own, James held the wheel at the helm and turned the ship in gentle curves. He stepped back, almost afraid, then gradually pulled one lever and pushed the other. The stars spun as the ship corkscrewed through space. James laughed and the ship was sent wheeling, ducking, diving, rising, somersaulting. His feet stayed on the deck, for there is no up in space, and the ship's ether held him down.

A short while later and he frowned. James ran to the back railing and leant over. Three rudders – one twice as long as the others and vertical, and the other two horizontal – stuck out from either side of the ship. Satisfied, James finished his walk around the ship, noticing small details and slight imperfections.

Goggles on, James stood again by the bowsprit and took in the ship. The ether pushed the sails taut in waves of differing strength so one might notice a slight rocking. A slight wind tugged his hair. He took from his pocket the small arrowhead inscribed with silver that Artemis had given him. He looked out, to the stars where they were headed. *Best,* he thought, *I throw this away.*

Quiet footsteps broke his reverie. It was Giles, pipe in hand, eyes shining as he, too, took it all in.

"Captain, I was just about to retire when I noticed her turn, somersault, and almost all else." Giles nodded to the goggles hanging around his neck. "I see you found a pair of spacer goggles."

"Reg gave them to me." James tucked the arrowhead back in his pocket. "Spacer goggles, that makes sense. How are Milo and Freya doing?"

"Aye lad, captain, they're doing all right. Resting, like I thought you would be."

"Reg dragged me out here. I had to see it."

"Aye, it was worth waiting a thousand years to see this again."

James shivered at that sentence, said far too casually. "A thousand years? Why do you call me captain? You should be the captain, not me."

"You are the captain though, lad. It was Reg that chose it, all those years ago. Captain James Emerys."

"Captain James…" James shook his head. "Don't call me that. I've barely gotten my head 'round the fact I'm in space."

"All right, lad." Giles looked at him with kindly eyes. "For tonight I'll give you that. What else is on your mind?"

"This." James waved a hand at everything around him. "It's awesome. It's unbelievable, Giles. What have we got ourselves into?"

"An adventure, lad, with all the trouble and tribulations that come with a true adventure. It will change you, and there will be sorrow ahead, most likely. But lad, for what it's worth, you will never feel more alive."

James studied Giles: the many lines upon his face, his old clothes and calm air. "You waited for a thousand years? How is that even possible?"

"I am her Keeper. As long as I stay close to her" – Giles put a hand on the railing – "I won't die until she does, not of old age at least."

"A Keeper?"

"Aye, a Keeper of the Spirits. Spirits often don't interact well with us, lad. They either do too little, or far, far too much. Keepers protect them, and so in the long run protect everyone."

"That makes as much sense as the rest of this," James said. "Why were you waiting for a thousand years?"

"We" – Giles indicated the ship and himself – "were protecting Reg, as you know him. Waiting for him. Then when he was ready to take form, he found you, or you him. Gave me the biggest surprise in I don't know how long. Scared me half to death when he vanished that night."

"The night Reg and I met. You remember that?"

"Of course I do, lad." Giles smiled. "I was on the streets looking for him. Like, I imagine, your parents were for you. I came back and found you and him. I did not know what to do. Reg would not leave your side. I wouldn't keep you from your parents, so…"

"You left him with me."

"Yes."

"And you just accepted that the spirit you'd looked after for so long was now someone's pet."

"It was odd, although not the oddest thing I've seen a spirit do. It's not my place to question such things. I am just her Keeper. Although," Giles chuckled, "I admit I didn't expect Reg to do that. A strange way for a task of a thousand years to end."

James tried to imagine the time Giles had spent stuck on Earth. Centuries of looking up to the stars in vain.

Unable to, he said, "Sorry."

Giles looked at James in astonishment and laughed. "Lad, of all the people alive today, you are the last who should be apologising to me. Without you, I believe we would still be marooned, but now we are finally sailing the Aetherium again."

"I," James began, his mouth opening and closing. Then he shrugged. "I've got nothing. I don't know what to say to that."

"Lad, that's all right."

A few minutes of companionable silence and James asked, "What's out there, in the Aetherium?"

Giles kept his eyes on the vista before them, voice soft in remembrance. "In the two thousand years I've sailed, I have yet to see even a thousandth of the galaxy. There are species of every kind, some intelligent, others wild and a few monstrous. Fewer still, so peculiar they changed my understanding of what it is to be alive."

Giles leant forward, over the railing. "There are sights where seeing them will leave a mark on your soul. Planets of any and every description. The truth is, I don't know what's out there. It is more than I can describe, and more than any one person can imagine."

"I want that. To see all of that." James clutched the railing as if he could see those sights himself. A solar flare and the Aetherium rippled. "Are there other ships like this out there?"

"She might well be one of a kind by now, lad. But if you're talking about star ships, then yes."

James hesitated, unsure of how to say what he was thinking without sounding crazy.

"I can feel her, the ship, ever since we launched. Just there" – James waved a hand next to his ear – "and I could say hello."

"That's part of being her captain, lad. You're not going insane." Giles blew a smoke ring from his pipe. "Comes with the job."

"Thanks, guess that's solved then."

"When you are ready, lad, say hello. She's a fine, old lady once you get to know her."

James ran a hand through his hair. "That's a lot to get my head around."

"I can imagine."

The two lapsed once more into silence. One thought about the infinite possibilities which seemed to have leapt out of his wildest fantasies to reality. The other reminisced, his mind lost in the vast depths of his memories.

"Does she have a name?" James asked.

"Captain?"

"The ship, does she have a name?"

"Aye. I forgot to tell you, didn't I?" Giles chuckled. "Her name is *The Fury Rose*."

A leap of faith

A moment to change your life

So, jump my friends, jump

Trust your wings will catch you

For what is life without risk?

Without the ethereal winds against your skin, as you sail into the cosmos

What is life without a wee bit o' adventure?

Afterword

Thank you for reading my book. Hope you enjoyed this first step into the Aetherium as much as I did writing it.

If you like my writing, follow me on Instagram @poetry_of_emerys for more poems and news about my books. Or go to my website joseph-sheehan.com to continue to explore the lore and places of the Aetherium and join the mailing list to get updates on my writing, poems, and the universe of the Aetherium.

Trust me, you ain't seen nothing yet.

I started writing the first draft of this in 2016, and here it is available for others to read in 2023. The next one will not take so long, promise, and there will be a next one and many after that. Writing this helped me through some hard times, and so much happened during that time as well. Got married for one thing... =).

And finally, thank you to all those people who helped and supported me during this time. With a big shout out to my wife whose support was invaluable, Mum and Dad, all the friends who read the numerous other edits of this book. Also, to Jake Biggin and Amanda Rutter my illustrator and editor both of whom helped and gave advice long after they had too.

This book would not be what it is today without all the people I mentioned.

Please use the blank page, or pages, after this to doodle or draw what aliens and places James, Reg and the crew of The Fury Rose might journey too, or recreate a scene from the book, or just draw anything, anything at all. Write a poem, or a scene of your own book. Do whatever you like, these pages are blank because they are pages for you.

Printed in Great Britain
by Amazon